THE CASE OF THE
INSURANCE FRAUD
SACRIFICES

Volume 13: Zen and the Art of Investigation

ANTHONY WOLFF

authorHOUSE®

AuthorHouse™ LLC
1663 Liberty Drive
Bloomington, IN 47403
www.authorhouse.com
Phone: 1-800-839-8640

This is a work of fiction. All of the characters, names, incidents, organizations, and dialogue in this novel are either the products of the author's imagination or are used fictitiously.

Published by AuthorHouse 09/22/2014

ISBN: 978-1-4969-3291-4 (sc)
ISBN: 978-1-4969-3290-7 (e)

For T.R., J., and Ginger Crockett

PREFACE

WHO ARE THESE DETECTIVES ANYWAY?

"The eye cannot see itself" an old Zen adage informs us. The Private I's in these case files count on the truth of that statement. People may be self-concerned, but they are rarely self-aware.

In courts of law, guilt or innocence often depends upon its presentation. Juries do not - indeed, they may not - investigate any evidence in order to test its veracity. No, they are obliged to evaluate only what they are shown. Private Investigators, on the other hand, are obliged to look beneath surfaces and to prove to their satisfaction - not the court's - whether or not what appears to be true is actually true. The Private I must have a penetrating eye.

Intuition is a spiritual gift and this, no doubt, is why *Wagner & Tilson, Private Investigators* does its work so well.

At first glance the little group of P.I.s who solve these often baffling cases seem different from what we (having become familiar with video Dicks) consider "sleuths." They have no oddball sidekicks. They are not alcoholics. They get along well with cops.

George Wagner is the only one who was trained for the job. He obtained a degree in criminology from Temple University in Philadelphia and did exemplary work as a investigator with the Philadelphia Police. These were his golden years. He skied; he danced; he played tennis; he had a Porsche, a Labrador retriever, and a small sailboat. He got married and had a wife, two toddlers, and a house. He was handsome and well built, and he had great hair.

And then one night, in 1999, he and his partner walked into an ambush. His partner was killed and George was shot in the left knee and in his right shoulder's brachial plexus. The pain resulting from his injuries and the twenty-two surgeries he endured throughout the year that followed, left him addicted to a nearly constant morphine drip. By the time he was admitted to a rehab center in Southern California for treatment of his morphine addiction and for physical therapy, he had lost everything previously mentioned except his house, his handsome face, and his great hair.

His wife, tired of visiting a semi-conscious man, divorced him and married a man who had more than enough money to make child support payments unnecessary and, since he was the jealous type, undesirable. They moved far away, and despite the calls George placed and the money and gifts he sent, they soon tended to regard him as non-existent. His wife did have an orchid collection which she boarded with a plant nursery, paying for the plants' care until he was able to accept them. He gave his brother his car, his tennis racquets, his skis, and his sailboat.

At the age of thirty-four he was officially disabled, his right arm and hand had begun to wither slightly from limited use, a frequent result of a severe injury to that nerve center. His knee, too, was troublesome. He could not hold it in a bent position for an extended period of time; and when the weather was bad or he had been standing for too long, he limped a little.

George gave considerable thought to the "disease" of romantic love and decided that he had acquired an immunity to it. He would never again be vulnerable to its delirium. He did not realize that the gods of love regard such pronouncements as hubris of the worst kind and, as such, never allow it to go unpunished. George learned this lesson while working on the case, *The Monja Blanca*. A sweet girl, half his age and nearly half his weight, would fell him, as he put it, "as young David slew the big dumb Goliath." He understood that while he had no future with her, his future would be filled with her for as long as he had a mind that could think. She had been the victim of the most vicious swindlers he had ever encountered. They had successfully fled the country, but not the range of George's determination to apprehend them. These were master criminals, four of them, and he secretly vowed that he would make them fall, one by one. This was a serious quest. There was nothing quixotic about George Roberts Wagner.

While he was in the hospital receiving treatment for those fateful gunshot wounds, he met Beryl Tilson.

Beryl, a widow whose son Jack was then eleven years old, was working her way through college as a nurse's aid when she tended George. She had met him previously when he delivered a lecture on the curious differences between aggravated assault and attempted murder, a not uninteresting topic. During the year she tended him, they became friendly enough for him to communicate with her during the year he was in rehab. When he returned to Philadelphia, she picked him up at the airport, drove him home - to a house he had not been inside for two years - and helped him to get settled into a routine with the house and the botanical spoils of his divorce.

After receiving her degree in the Liberal Arts, Beryl tried to find a job with hours that would permit her to be home when her son came home from school each day. Her quest was daunting. Not only was a degree in Liberal Arts regarded as a 'negative' when considering an applicant's qualifications, (the choice of study having demonstrated a lack of foresight for eventual entry into the commercial job market) but by stipulating that she needed to be home no later than 3:30 p.m. each day, she further discouraged personnel managers from putting out their company's welcome mat. The supply of available jobs was somewhat limited.

Beryl, a Zen Buddhist and karate practitioner, was still doing part-time work when George proposed that they open a private investigation agency. Originally he had thought she would function as a "girl friday" office manager; but when he witnessed her abilities in the martial arts, which, at that time, far exceeded his, he agreed that she should function as a 50-50 partner in the agency, and he helped her through the licensing procedure. She quickly became an excellent marksman on the gun range.

As a Christmas gift he gave her a Beretta to use alternately with her Colt semi-automatic.

The Zen temple she attended was located on Germantown Avenue in a two storey, store-front row of small businesses. Wagner & Tilson, Private Investigators needed a home. Beryl noticed that a building in the same row was advertised for sale. She told George who liked it, bought it, and let Beryl and her son move into the second floor as their residence. Problem solved.

While George considered himself a man's man, Beryl did not see herself as a woman's woman. She had no female friends her own age. None. Acquaintances, yes. She enjoyed warm relationships with a few older women. But Beryl, it surprised her to realize, was a man's woman. She liked men, their freedom to move, to create, to discover, and that inexplicable wildness that came with their physical presence and strength. All of her senses found them agreeable; but she had no desire to domesticate one. Going to sleep with one was nice. But waking up with one of them in her bed? No. No. No. Dawn had an alchemical effect on her sensibilities. "Colors seen by candlelight do not look the same by day," said Elizabeth Barrett Browning, to which Beryl replied, "Amen."

She would find no occasion to alter her orisons until, in the course of solving a missing person's case that involved sexual slavery in a South American rainforest, a case called *Skyspirit*, she met the Surinamese Southern District's chief criminal investigator. Dawn became conducive to romance. But, as we all know, the odds are always against the success of long distance love affairs. To be stuck in one continent and love a man who is stuck in another holds as much promise for high romance as falling in love with Dorian Gray. In her professional life, she was tough but fair. In matters of lethality, she preferred *dim mak* points to bullets, the latter being awfully messy.

Perhaps the most unusual of the three detectives is Sensei Percy Wong. The reader may find it useful to know a bit more about his background.

Sensei, Beryl's karate master, left his dojo to go to Taiwan to become a fully ordained Zen Buddhist priest in the Ummon or Yun Men lineage in which he was given the Dharma name Shi Yao Feng. After studying advanced martial arts in both Taiwan and China, he returned to the U.S. to teach karate again and to open a small Zen Buddhist temple - the temple that was down the street from the office *Wagner & Tilson* would eventually open.

Sensei was quickly considered a great martial arts' master not because, as he explains, "I am good at karate, but because I am better at advertising it." He was of Chinese descent and had been ordained in China, and since China's Chan Buddhism and Gung Fu stand in polite rivalry to Japan's Zen Buddhism and Karate, it was most peculiar to find a priest in China's Yun Men lineage who followed the Japanese Zen liturgy and the martial arts discipline of Karate.

It was only natural that Sensei Percy Wong's Japanese associates proclaimed that his preferences were based on merit, and in fairness to them, he did not care to disabuse them of this notion. In truth, it was Sensei's childhood rebellion against his tyrannical faux-Confucian father that caused him to gravitate to the Japanese forms. Though both of his parents had emigrated from China, his father decried western civilization even as he grew rich exploiting its freedoms and commercial opportunities. With draconian finesse he imposed upon his family the cultural values of the country from which he had fled for his life. He seriously believed that while the rest of the world's population might have come out of Africa, Chinese men came out of heaven. He did not know or care where Chinese women originated so long as they kept their proper place as slaves.

His mother, however, marveled at American diversity and refused to speak Chinese to her children, believing, as she did, in the old fashioned idea that it is wise to speak the language of the country in which one claims citizenship.

At every turn the dear lady outsmarted her obsessively sinophilic husband. Forced to serve rice at every meal along with other mysterious creatures obtained in Cantonese Chinatown, she purchased two Shar Peis that, being from Macau, were given free rein of the dining room. These dogs, despite their pre-Qin dynasty lineage, lacked a discerning palate and proved to be gluttons for bowls of fluffy white stuff. When her husband retreated to his rooms, she served omelettes and Cheerios, milk instead of tea, and at dinner, when he was not there at all, spaghetti instead of chow mein. The family home was crammed with gaudy enameled furniture and torturously carved teak; but on top of the lion-head-ball-claw-legged coffee table, she always placed a book which illustrated the elegant simplicity of such furniture designers as Marcel Breuer; Eileen Gray; Charles Eames; and American Shakers. Sensei adored her; and loved to hear her relate how, when his father ordered her to give their firstborn son a Chinese name; she secretly asked the clerk to record indelibly the name "Percy" which she mistakenly thought was a very American name. To Sensei, if she had named him Abraham Lincoln Wong, she could not have given him a more Yankee handle.

Preferring the cuisines of Italy and Mexico, Sensei avoided Chinese food and prided himself on not knowing a word of Chinese. He balanced this ignorance by an inability to understand Japanese and, because of its inaccessibility, he did not eat Japanese food.

The Man of Zen who practices Karate obviously is the adventurous type; and Sensei, staying true to type, enjoyed participating in Beryl's and George's investigations. It required little time for him to become a one-third partner of the team. He called himself, "the ampersand in *Wagner & Tilson.*"

Sensei Wong may have been better at advertising karate than at performing it, but this merely says that he was a superb huckster for the discipline. In college he had studied civil engineering; but he also was on the fencing team and he regularly practiced gymnastics. He had learned yoga and ancient forms of meditation from his mother. He attained Zen's vaunted transcendental states which he could access 'on the mat.' It was not surprising that when he began to learn karate he was already half-accomplished. After he won a few minor championships he attracted the attention of several martial arts publications that found his "unprecedented" switchings newsworthy. They imparted to him a "great master" cachet, and perpetuated it to the delight of dojo owners and martial arts shopkeepers. He did win many championships and, through unpaid endorsements and political propaganda, inspired the sale of Japanese weapons, including nunchaku and shuriken which he did not actually use.

Although his Order was strongly given to celibacy, enough wiggle room remained for the priest who found it expedient to marry or dally. Yet, having reached his mid-forties unattached, he regarded it as 'unlikely' that he would ever be romantically welded to a female, and as 'impossible' that he would be bonded to a citizen and custom's agent of the People's Republic of China - whose Gung Fu abilities challenged him and who would strike terror in his heart especially when she wore Manolo Blahnik red spike heels. Such combat, he insisted, was patently unfair, but he prayed that Providence would not level the playing field. He met his femme fatale while working on *A Case of Virga*.

Later in their association Sensei would take under his spiritual wing a young Thai monk who had a degree in computer science and a flair for acting. Akara Chatree, to whom Sensei's master in Taiwan would give the name Shi Yao Xin, loved Shakespeare; but his father - who came from one of Thailand's many noble families - regarded his son's desire to become an actor as we would regard our son's desire to become a hit man. Akara's brothers were all businessmen and professionals; and as the old patriarch lay dying, he exacted a promise from his tall 'matinee-idol' son that he would never tread upon the flooring of a stage. The old man had asked for nothing else, and since he bequeathed a rather large sum of money to his young son, Akara had to content himself with critiquing the performances of actors who were less filially constrained than he. As far as romance is concerned, he had not thought too much about it until he worked on *A Case of Industrial Espionage*. That case took him to Bermuda, and what can a young hero do when he is captivated by a pretty girl who can recite Portia's lines with crystalline insight while lying beside him on a white beach near a blue ocean?

But his story will keep...

WHO IS AKARA CHATREE (SHI QIAN FA)?

It could be argued, and frequently was, that Akara Chatree's solitary personality had been occasioned by his having inherited a considerable amount of money, so much so that less affluent persons - which included all of his associates at the time that he was financially blessed - pestered him so relentlessly to lend them money or to invest in their business ventures, that for the sake of his sanity he was driven to eschew all "friendships." But this would not be true.

It was also suspected that when he realized that the degree of difference between his intelligence and the common man's was many times greater than the difference between the common man's and the ape's, he was forced into a peculiar taxonomic niche, one in which he could "interbreed" socially and sexually with only those individuals who were similarly endowed. This was a ludicrous surmise.

And then it was supposed that he had "taken up the cloth" because he had spiritual ambitions which only the hermit's life could accommodate. Yet, he chose to be a priest rather than a monk, a choice which belied a preference for isolation.

Akara Chatree had simply been purged of the human tendency to assign values to groups of people. He was convinced that beyond saying some five or six billion individuals occupied the earth, no further qualitative descriptions of the psychological sort could be applied. He therefore limited his interactions to specific persons, persons that he could trust and appreciate for their integrity and kindness. He avoided parties, assemblies, and gatherings of any kind that would subject him to the vagaries of strangers.

Bold assertions such as these are not made in the glacial tempo of evolution. They are the stuff of a revolutionary *coup*. All of a man's channels of opinion must be diverted and directed to engage the turbines of a new uber-view generator, a vantage point that encompasses all universals.

Akara Chatree's revolution occurred when he was fourteen years old. As a child he had casually accepted those class distinctions which served to maintain his family's social position. He was told that the members of his family were judicious and responsible because of their inherent sense of *Noblesse Oblige*. Money, he was assured, had nothing to do with it. Attending private schools in England did not dull the blade of class division.

And then when he was fourteen his "dominion" class made a trip to India to attend a *puja* in Bihar and to tour the state. Akara, the only child of his father's second marriage, expected to meet with four of his half-brothers, sons of his father's first and third marriages. All of Akara's relatives, with the exception of his mother, lived in Thailand, and Bihar was not considered a distant place.

Shortly after the class arrived in India, all three chaperones and half of the student group were stricken with an intestinal disturbance, leaving the hardy half of the young tourists, which included Akara and a school friend, without much in the way of supervision. His half-brothers, however, were chaperoned by a Draconian Theravadin Buddhist uncle.

Told that several pornographic films were going to be shown in a nearby town, Akara, his brothers and his school friend arranged to meet outside the theater. More than familial enjoyment was involved in the reunion. Akara's friend had borrowed money from him to pay a gambling debt which he had not taken seriously until he was beaten senseless by a debt collector. He had not wanted his parents to know the truth of his loss, and so he begged Akara not only to lend him the repayment money but to keep secret its purpose. Akara obliged and asked his older half-brothers if they would lend him five-thousand pounds so that he could pay a personal debt. Akara's friend had promised to give him a substantial part of the repayment when they met at the theater.

As they sneaked away to the town, a late and heavy rain was falling; and just as they assembled, a levee broke and the boys were separated in the ensuing muddy flood. Akara was carried by the current until finally he found himself buried waist-deep in mud from which he could not extricate himself. His school friend heard and acknowledged his cries for help and told his brothers where he was, and then he left. None of them came to help Akara or to direct any of the official rescue personnel to his location.

His brothers had run from the area because they did not want their uncle to learn where they had been and why they had been there. His friend, he realized, had seen a financial opportunity. With Akara dead - as he was sure he would be since so many others in the path of the flood had already perished - he would be relieved of having to repay the debt.

All night, Akara shivered and whimpered, distraught by his abandonment. Towards dawn, a man who cleaned out cesspools for a living began to use his tools to dig a circle around him. The man refused to look in Akara's face or even to speak to him. He simply dug until enough of the thick mud was removed. Then he pulled the exhausted boy out of the morass, put him on a kind of pontoon raft, and poled his way to firm land. He refused to accept money for his efforts, and only after Akara repeatedly asked him his name, did he finally mumble what sounded like "Kyamay Apkimadah."

As he lay Akara on the doorstep of a medical facility, a villager came and hit the man with a broom handle and told Akara to bathe carefully with Ganga River water since his body had made contact with an Untouchable.

It was on that night that Akara Chatree gained his world-view. He did not return to England but instead went directly to Sao Paulo where his mother met him at the airport and took him home to the building that housed her Zen Buddhist Center.

In a room that measured two meters by three meters, he had a bed, a closet, a desk, a lamp, and courtesy of the last man who occupied the room, six books: an English dictionary; the complete works of William Shakespeare; three mathematics books that took him through intermediate and advanced Calculus; and a first year University text in Physics. The bathroom was at the end of the hall. The kitchen was downstairs. Akara went nowhere else for nearly two years — and two hundred books later. When he did emerge from the Center, it was to matriculate at the University. He only agreed to go there because he wanted to master computer science and needed access to the equipment. (Shakespeare he knew and understood far better than any and all members of the English Department.) He had no friends or enemies and he neither carried a cellphone nor accepted visitors at his Zen Center residence. He was pleasant and cooperative, but he said nothing that did not need to be said.

He had one quirk. On the flyleaf of every book he bought from the date beginning with the mudslide, he wrote the name (as he remembered it) of the man who had helped him. *Kyamay Apkimadah*

Akara was twenty-three years old and working on his PhD in Computer Science before he learned from a Sanskrit professor that no doubt the words that had been spoken to him were not anyone's name, but simple Hindi for "I help you."

Kyā maiṁ āpakī madada. क्या मैं आपकी मदद.

That night, in 2007, Akara Chatree cried for several hours and then asked his mother to prepare him to take Holy Orders. He became the Zen Buddhist priest, Shi Qian Fa of the Yun Men (Ummon) lineage.

In China he mentioned to his master that he did not want to join the clerical staff of a large business-like temple. He was therefore directed to the little Zen temple on Germantown Avenue, in Philadelphia, and in 2012 he became an assistant to his master's old friend, Sensei Percy Wong (Shi Yao Feng). He moved into the second floor of the temple along with his sixteen server cluster of computer "stuff." He also rented a garage nearby so that he could park his new bright red Corvette inside it.

Eventually, he obtained his private investigator's license. This is the first case about which he could unequivocally say that he "worked on."

TUESDAY, OCTOBER 2, 2012

George Wagner cursed himself for not following the great Dao Master's advice, "If you want to attract someone, take a step backwards." He had stepped forward, and now he realized that he forced away the woman he had hoped would come closer.

Baltimore is a much more advantageous location for a Philadelphia-based courtship than Manila; and by an inverse proportion of that same degree, George's normal *savoir faire* had dumbed itself down into schoolboy awkwardness.

He had been so excited when Dr. Carla Richards told him that she was coming to Maryland to take a year's worth of medical refresher courses that he forgot that ancient wisdom. He drove to Baltimore to meet her plane as it came in from the Philippines. He took her to a motel near the University Medical School and, because he knew that she was short of money, he paid for her first week's lodging and would have paid for more if she had allowed him. He went with her to the book store when she got the expensive texts she needed and he gave the cashier his credit card before she could object. He had lunch with her in the Student Union cafeteria and told her he'd gladly buy her a new, inexpensive small car, but she had refused. He then called his partner Beryl Tilson and asked if she would drive down in her "extra" family car to let Carla temporarily use it.

Beryl, who had spoken frequently to Carla but had never met her, was happy to drive down, meet the two of them for dinner, and then to drive back to Philadelphia with George in his pickup truck.

Carla was not a U.S. citizen, and not even credit card companies were eager to let her "buy now, pay later." She could rationalize accepting help

5

since she could not attain her goal without it. But gratitude is a weak, unstable thing compared to pride. It is porous and quickly soaks up pride's oozing suspicions about the giver's motives. Love and kindness become the constituents of exploitation, and as such, must be resisted and resented.

It happened that on that first day, while George and Carla were eating lunch in the student cafeteria, she noticed a bulletin board advertisement for a house-sitter in Dalton Creek, a rural town just north of Baltimore. The next evening, when George called her at the motel to ask if she needed anything that he could help her with, her voice rippled enthusiastically over the news. She had contacted a "very nice man" who had placed an ad she had seen, and she would be driving to the town for an interview with him the next evening. "The town's location is perfect," she said. "There's a highway that goes directly down to the medical school. And my duties at the house would be minimal. I'd have plenty of time to study."

George issued a caveat about moving into the residences of strangers. "Let me check this guy out," he said. He could hear her liquid tone freeze at the suggestion. In fact her whole throat seemed to have frosted-over as she managed to say, "I really don't think that's necessary."

George, still remembering the intimate week they spent together sailing on the South China Sea, offered, "I can come down this weekend and stay from Saturday noon until Sunday afternoon. We can look the place over."

Carla regretted that she was not available to spend what she was certain would be a lovely visit with him. She casually explained that mutual friends of theirs, Dwight Ingram and his daughter Chloe, were coming down from Lake George, New York for the weekend. Dwight had paid the tuition for her med school refresher courses and for her plane fare from the Philippines. Naturally, she would have to give them her full attention.

George, feeling the twinge of an old jealousy of Dwight Ingram, asked her to give them his regards, and then added that she should not hesitate to charge another week of living at the motel to him. "The manager can call me for verification if he needs to."

Carla immediately replied, "That is really sweet of you but if things go as I hope, I'll either be moving into that house in Dalton Creek or becoming another student's roommate. *I'll call you* to let you know how things are going."

George felt the stab of "I'll call you," and his euphoria deflated. He came down to earth in what could not be called "a three point landing." The romance had crashed, he thought, and, especially in view of Dwight Ingram's involvement in the mishap, he doubted that the mangled mess could ever be repaired.

He grew sullen and didn't want to talk to or about Carla again. Beryl noticed that this refusal did not jibe with the way he quickly reached for his private phone to answer it. "You look like one of those jilted lovers," she said, "who call the other up to say, 'I'm calling to tell you not to call me any more.'"

"You ought to start an 'Advice to the Lovelorn' column," George said. "Your first ten inquiries will come from someone named Beryl. After you straighten those out, I'll send you mine."

THURSDAY, OCTOBER 4, 2012

In Dalton Creek, Maryland, Carla sat in the pleasant living room of Roland and Sybil Melbourne and chatted casually about a subject that had destroyed her home and family: Mount Pinatubo's 1991 catastrophic eruption.

"I grew up seeing that mountain every day. I knew what a danger it was. At the time of the devastating eruption, I was in undergraduate school in Arizona," she related, "and heard of the event on the news. For days I could get no information, and when I did get it, the tragedy still came as a shock. Everyone in my family, with the exception of my mother, was killed; and the farmland my family had occupied for decades was inundated with the toxic ash and mud from the pyroclastic flows. My mother never recovered emotionally. She literally had nowhere to go so I brought her back with me and she stayed until I received my medical degree. I had wanted to continue on with a surgical residency, but she so longed to return to the Philippines that I had to forego this intention and take her back to the few friends and relatives she had left in Luzon.

"Now," Carla concluded, "my career is on track again. I'm taking refresher courses in medicine so that I can qualify for a surgical residency. It's been twenty-one years since Pinatubo erupted and fifteen years since my plans to become a surgeon were derailed. I thank God that everything seems to be getting back on track."

"Did your mother find the happiness she sought when she returned?" Sybil asked.

"No, not really. She had been in Manila the day of the catastrophe, and she had the idée fixe that somehow she was to blame for having gone to Manila to buy a special dress for some social function. God had punished her vanity. She was guilty of not being home to save the rest of the family."

"You are entitled to much good fortune," Sybil nodded sympathetically.

"Well," Roland said, standing and gesturing that Carla follow him, "before we get to the standard employment contract," he showed her a form that was so titled, "we need to show you your accommodations. Once we have your approval we can proceed."

At the far end of the second floor hall, a wooden pull-down ladder waited for them to climb it. "I detest these things," Roland said as he indicated that Carla should precede him up the stairs.

As her eyes cleared the floor level she could see the apartment in the shadowy light the moon supplied as it shone through the dormer windows. She waited at the stair's landing as Roland lit a lamp that filled a corner of the room with a soft glow. He walked across the room and lit two other bright lamps. "Do you like it?" he asked.

Carla gasped at the large room that was so clean and tastefully furnished. "What is there not to like? I adore Danish modern furniture." She opened a closet door. "My goodness," she gushed. "It's bigger than some of the dorm rooms I've lived in!" Roland laughed.

"And I see that you've got two fire extinguishers!" Her eye immediately noticed the absence of an escape ladder. "Excuse me," she said softly, "but there seems to be only one way to exit the apartment — down those wooden stairs. Shouldn't there be an escape mechanism? What if there's a fire—"

"Good Lord!" Roland whispered as he plopped down on the couch. "I apologize. I was supposed to have taken care of this and I've had so much on my mind lately, I completely forgot. You shall not sleep for five minutes in this apartment until the escape ladder is installed. I'll order it tomorrow and insist that it be installed immediately. Please, Carla, please don't let my negligence dissuade you from accepting the position. You are precisely the person we're looking for. Please sit down a moment and let me explain the real reason that your placement here is... well... vital."

Carla sat beside him on the couch. "It is true," he began, "that having a person on the premises at all times, or as least as much as possible, does deter crime. But I have another reason. My son Barry has just started college. I confess that his mother and I despaired that he'd ever free himself from his wild teenage friends who had developed what they feel is a philosophical response to the modern age's materialism. If they had their way, they'd sit around all day, smoking weed and arguing about Bertrand Russell - as if they ever understood Bertrand Russell any better than I did after four years at university. They can't tolerate authority figures to be within five hundred yards of them, and they absolutely refuse to enter this house when an adult is home. It doesn't matter which adult... our maid, the gardener, my wife or I, the caterer, an encyclopedia salesman, anyone. To be perfectly honest, a couple of them are on probation, and a call to the police would put them back in jail.

"My son Barrington - we call him Barry - is a good kid and he likes people. If he's home alone and a few of them show up... he'll let them in and then nothing but trouble comes. They eat us out of house and home. If they find a pie in the freezer, they'll bake it. I've even known them to barbecue steaks outside in the winter time. Needless to say, inside the house the place winds up smelling of marijuana. But if someone is here, and they see a car in the driveway, they just keep on going.

"Also, I don't think I mentioned that I have two elderly spinster aunts who live down the road. You'd have to look in on them from time to time. Just pop in and say, 'Hello.' It's common knowledge that I'm an accountant and often travel to my company's various branches. My wife, however, has recently accepted a position as a real estate appraiser - in commercial real estate. These appraisals sometimes take days to complete and can be in distant parts of the state. So what we need and want is to have a responsible person here in the house on any night that Barry is home. He generally stays in his apartment near his school in Hagerstown - that's about seventy-five miles from here - so what I'm asking is that you let your presence protect the house, so to speak. Barry is our only child."

"I was wondering why the job was such a good deal. Now I understand. I'm glad you explained."

"But I have two favors I must insist upon."

"Which are?"

"The first is that you don't let it get out that you're functioning as a teenage boy's Nanny or chaperone or concierge or guard. What I told you must remain our secret."

"I understand. Your son would think that you're spying on him and he'd resent it."

"Exactly. And the second thing... and this is an absolute! You cannot tell my wife that I forgot to get the emergency ladder. She will kill me!" He began to laugh. "Ah, if only I were joking!"

Carla laughed too.

The standard employment contract contained a confidentiality agreement. Roland winked at Carla as he pointed to it. "We've had people who worked in our home who then went to the bar or the beauty parlor and discussed information they gathered from documents lying about... my firm's clients... my intention to bid on a certain property... how much my wife paid for an evening gown. Oh yes! This Agreement simply requires you to not disclose any information whatsoever that you acquire in the course of your employment here."

"It sounds like a reasonable request. Preventing gossip is undoubtedly the best way to deal with it. Of course, I'm happy to comply."

Roland called neighbors Charles and Agnes Merriweather to come to the Melbourne house to witness the contract's execution.

"Can you move your things in this weekend?" Sybil asked. "It's a long weekend since Monday is a holiday, Columbus Day. We'll come and help you transport your things."

"You can borrow my pickup," Charles Merriweather offered.

"No," Carla said graciously, "I really don't have that much to transport. I'll be here on Friday... after class."

The house was lovely. The people were refined. The salary was excellent. The location was perfect. After years of elaborate disappointments and plain bad luck, Carla's life was finally delivering on solid promises and good fortune. Who could have asked for a better job?

She lay upon her bed in the motel and grinned at her contract. The fine print that she had ignored now appeared in a larger font and she read that even discussing the fact that she had signed a confidentiality agreement was confidential unless her testimony was being compelled by a court. If she broke the agreement she could be sued for damages that were not less than fifty-thousand dollars, and in addition to this, she would be liable for all the legal costs of the employer.

This information disturbed her and she wanted to ask someone about it. But she was already prohibited from doing that. "I need to do my own thinking," she said. "If I don't gossip, I have nothing to worry about. I'll be careful about the information I share."

Satisfied that she could maintain her discretion, she called George, as promised, to let him know the results of her interview. The enthusiasm she felt for her new job added warmth to her voice.

Effusively, she reported, "They've finished the entire attic. There's even a bathroom up there, and it's all for my use. It has its own air conditioner and heating unit; it gets the morning sun; and the view from the dormer windows is spectacular. A maid comes in three mornings a week to clean house and do the laundry. And I have full kitchen privileges - but they have a gourmet catering service that delivers dinner late every afternoon, so I can eat alone or wait to eat with Roland and his wife in the dining room. And get this! I get paid $300 a week. I can hardly believe it!"

"What are your duties?" he asked warily.

Carla immediately regretted calling George. She did not know what she was permitted to reveal and what she had agreed to keep secret. She decided that she could trust George with general information. "I'm to house-sit at night... just be on the premises. His business often takes him away from home for days at a time, and so does his wife's. They want someone reliable in the house every night. They have a son, but he's away in college. Roland does have elderly aunts who live less than a kilometer down the road. Occasionally, I'll have to look in on them."

"Why don't they just get a home alarm system? It isn't as if burglaries and fires don't occur during the day when there's nobody home."

Her reluctance to answer gave her voice a petulance she did not intend. "There's nothing like the physical presence of a resident to deter criminals."

George, a former police investigator, was happy to receive the information. He decided not to say, "Unless the criminal is a rapist." Carla was a beautiful woman and like beautiful people everywhere, her attractive features imbued her with an exaggerated sense of power. "I don't know, Carla," he said cautiously. "It sounds like one of those 'too good to be true' deals. Are you sure you don't want me to check these people out?"

"I'm positive," she said and abruptly changed the subject. "Roland says he wants to help me get a new car, but in the meantime, I'd like to keep Beryl's car for another couple of weeks or so. Would that be all right?"

"Sure. She keeps it in my garage for her son to use when he's in town. He won't be home until Thanksgiving--"

"–I'll be sure to get it back to Philadelphia long before that."

He was glad she cut him off before he had a chance to say that he and Beryl could come down at any time to pick up the car. Having to decline his offer would have discomfited them both.

George Wagner retreated. He did not call Carla again because it offended him to think that that she was interpreting his acts of friendship as acts that constituted romantic obligation. He also did not know how to call her. She had given him neither of her new numbers, residential or cellphone, and she had apparently intended to keep him from learning them since the "caller identification" function on his phone's screen was mute on the subject. Well, he had a bellyful of women using him and then making him feel like an overreaching fool. Enough was enough.

Instead of worrying about Dr. Carla Richards, George decided to devote himself to helping Akara Chatree, the young Zen Buddhist priest who lived and worked in the Temple down the street, to study for his private investigator's license. George admired the young priest's intelligence and wit and enjoyed mentoring him in the various aspects of investigation.

SATURDAY, OCTOBER 6, 2012

Carla had been almost too excited to sleep. "I have been so blessed!" she whispered, and she prayed for the first time in five years. The night was crisp and clear and she could look up from her pillow and see the stars through the window. An owl had chosen the branch of an oak tree that stood tall enough to claim the view of one of the dormer windows. The bird hooed and hooted, giving field mice ample warning. She didn't hear him leave. She noticed only the silence he left behind.

At breakfast with Sybil and Roland, she learned how to arm and disarm the house's periphery security system. "It's an old system," Roland explained, "but it's adequate for our needs." He took her to the front steps. "There," he pointed to a rock that was a different shade of grey from the rocks around it, "is a phony rock that holds a key to the front door - if you ever find yourself locked out."

He showed her the garage. "It's only a two car garage. Barrington parks his yellow Mustang on the side lawn and I'm afraid that you'll have to park your car there as well. The maid comes Monday, Wednesday, and Friday - in the mornings, when we're not at home. She just parks in the driveway. I'm telling you this because in a couple of hours some friends will be dropping by to meet you and they'll be parking all over the place. You've already met Charles and Agnes Merriweather. There'll also be a few other neighbors and some people from work. You may find yourself answering the phone from time to time... and it's nice to know to whom you're speaking... nice for them and nice for you."

Carla quickly changed her clothing. Her suit was wrinkled but, she was delighted to see, an ironing board and iron were in the apartment waiting to be used. When she descended the wooden staircase, she was made up and smartly dressed.

Roland whispered in her ear, "I'm going to say something that you never heard me say. You look beautiful." She giggled slightly as he presented a guest to her. "Carla, may I present the Perle Mesta of Dalton Creek, Frances Durwood Dalton. Frances, our houseguest, Dr. Carla Richards."

"Don't pay any attention to him," Frances warned. "I'm merely the 'go to' person in these parts. So, tell me about yourself."

Roland excused himself to accede to his wife's request that he go down to the basement and bring up more serving dishes and napkins for the canapes. A door in the dining room stood open, and when Roland entered it, Carla knew that this was the basement door. Her attention returned to Frances Durwood Dalton. "What," the guest asked, "brings you to these parts?"

"I'm taking refresher courses in anatomy, physiology, and histology - and *history* as well as *histology* since I'll have to be tested in medical jurisprudence in order to meet Maryland's licensing requirements."

"Well, you have come to the right place if it's history you're interested in. Roland's two spinster aunts, Winifred and Daphne Buehler - down the road a piece - are living Revolutionary War relics. Their house is stuffed with authentic Americana... furniture, colonial implements, even a decade's worth of Poor Richard's Almanack. And they can give you details about every item."

"It sounds like a wonderful collection," Carla said.

"I don't know if you could buy a small country for what its worth, but if you got a good agent you might be able to make a sizable down payment on one." She looked around. "Roland," she called, "where are your aunts?"

"At home, I hope," he replied. "They're becoming more reclusive and distrustful of strangers."

"Old age will do that to you," Agnes Merriweather chimed in.

TUESDAY, OCTOBER 9, 2012

Roland took time off from work so that he could escort Carla to the Department of Motor Vehicles to get her Maryland driver's license and then to a local bank to open her own checking account. At one o'clock he dropped her off at the house. She used her own key to unlock the front door and immediately punched the code into the vestibule's security keypad, closed the front door, and pressed the key that re-activated the alarm system. It was the first time that she was alone in the house.

She went up to her attic apartment to change her clothes, and then decided to inspect the house superficially... to learn how many rooms it had... what, in general terms, the rooms were used for, what the routes for escape were in the event of fire, and so on.

Wearing tennis shoes and jeans, she descended the pull-down staircase, and began to explore the second floor.

All the doors, she noticed, were shut. She went to the far end of the hall and opened the first door which led into the master bedroom. Not being the prying kind, she did not enter the room, but she did look far enough into it to see a large private bathroom attached to it.

She reentered the hallway, closed the door and went to the next door which opened to reveal a guest bedroom. No bathroom was attached. The next room was the common-use bathroom with stall shower and tub and linen closet. The next room was clearly Barry's. There were pennants on the wall, Pin-up girl and heavy metal posters... a nicely framed poster of Jimi Hendrix. Just as she began to step back into the hall, her glance fell upon a cluster of prescription bottles that stood on top of a chest of drawers. She saw and recognized prescriptions for propranolol, modafinil, disulfiram and several other medications. Startled, she had known these drugs to be used mostly to treat addiction withdrawal. She examined the bottles more closely and saw that the prescriptions had been written by several physicians over a two year period.

She thought that she had a right to be annoyed by Roland's failure to disclose the true nature of Barry's problems, but, on the other hand, it helped to explain the confidentiality agreement. Roland, like most fathers, would not care to have his son's troubles become the subject of gossip. She replaced the bottles and exited the room. The door to the last room on the floor revealed a small bedroom that was used for sewing and storage.

Downstairs she continued her exploration of the house. The stairs had emptied into the large living room with which she was already familiar. The dining room also offered no mystery. She came to a door which bore the sign, Office. She was not surprised to find that the door was locked. "Ah," she told herself, "I'd lock it, too, if I had to contend with undisciplined kids running around."

Opposite the office were a small solarium that was filled with plants and the door to the cellar. This door had stood open during the impromptu party. She tried to turn the knob but found the door locked. This puzzled her since, during her party, Roland had gotten wine from a large rack in the kitchen. The door did not open into a wine cellar that needed to be guarded from teenage raiders.

Another security keypad was located near the exterior kitchen door. She punched in the disarming code and went outside to look at the grounds in the afternoon sun. The house, she estimated, sat on about an acre of land... maybe more. There was a copse of trees - oak, maple, and some evergreens - at the rear of the property. The tree line continued to a distant house which, she assumed, was the Buehler house. She followed a footpath that led back to the trees and saw that it ended at an overgrown bridal path that seemed to connect both properties.

As she returned to the house she noticed a mail truck drive past the house without stopping to put any mail in the mailbox. She knew from experience that most people get mail on Monday, or definitely Tuesday, if Monday was a holiday. Why didn't they?

She returned to the house and rearmed the security system.

While she opened kitchen drawers and cabinet doors, the doorbell rang. She went to the front door and, looking through the peephole, saw a uniformed man carrying a insulated tray. "Who is it?" she called.

"The caterer, Ma'am. I left the new code back in the truck. Thought I'd ask you to save me the trouble of getting it."

"New code?" She asked, opening the door and keying in the code.

"Sure. It's required after every new addition or subtraction to the residential roll. You're an addition to the premises. The code was changed." He stepped inside, carrying a large insulated bag. "Dinner for three!"

"Ah, I see," Carla acknowledged the information. "I guess I just used the new code. And yes, dinner for three."

Within the hour, Roland and Sybil returned, and as the three diners sat at the table, the mystery of the mail was solved. Roland picked up the mail at the post office. "It's on my way home from work," he explained. "But sometimes," he added, "when I have to work late, Sybil will pick it up."

As they sipped coffee, Roland brought a stack of letters to the table and removed the rubber band that bound them. He shuffled through the mail, extracting items that were intended for Carla - her laminated driver's license and some promotional literature from the bank.

"I think," he announced, "that it's time Carla went to the Buehler house to meet my aunts. I know I should have attended to this sooner, but I've been so busy what with the emergency escape ladder's installation, the DMV, and the bank. But we really can't put it off much longer. How about if we take a walk down there on Saturday?"

"I look forward to it," Carla replied.

SATURDAY, OCTOBER 13, 2012

"Before we go to my Aunts' house, I have to go to a pet shop. There's no secret about my aunts' senile ways. They are a couple of eccentric old ladies who can't quite determine which century they're living in. But I thought I would kill two birds with one stone, so to speak. They need something to occupy their minds - I was reading about this in a magazine article. They always loved dogs, but never replaced the last one they had that died. He was a rather bumptious fellow, a cocky cocker spaniel. Always barking and always jumping on you. That was many years ago when Winifred wasn't suffering from Retinitis pigmentosa and Daphne didn't have osteoarthritis. Only an extremely small dog would be safe to bring into their home. I found just such a dog... a chihuahua. It's not a puppy... but eight months old is not an adult either. Are you allergic to animal hair?" Roland asked.

"No," Carla said. "And I think a chihuahua would be perfect for two ladies to make a fuss over."

"They're becoming so forgetful that I have to be extra careful. There was a home invasion in the area a few nights ago, and my aunts are frightened. As I've said, they're a couple of old spinsters who worry about boogie men hiding in the closet. I'd like you to stay with them for a few days and to make you a more acceptable housemate than you already are - as if that were possible - I'll let you present them with the doggie. Don't worry about your dinner. I'll bring it down myself. They use the same caterer, so there will be no problem, time-wise. I'll see to it that your dinner is delivered in time for you to eat with them. Also, take a laundry bag with you in case you have to stay longer. We pay our laundress to do

19

your things. My aunts pay their laundress to do their things. It wouldn't be fair to make one employee do the work that we pay another to do."

Carla wanted to say, "Why not let me pay their laundress extra to do mine?" but she decided not to voice the suggestion. This job was just too good to risk making suggestions that could be construed as criticisms. Instead she said, "Yes, it would probably do them good to get some exercise walking the dog."

In half an hour, Roland returned with a dog-carrying box. "Shall we go?" he asked. Sybil stayed at home and waved to them as they walked down the footpath towards the trees.

"I should explain," Roland said, "there was an argument about putting in a sidewalk. As you can see, the lawns go right down to the street, which, until a few years ago, was a dirt road. On the other side of the street, there is a sidewalk. We have always maintained that one is not necessary since we use the bridal path. The truth is that my aunts do not want strangers traipsing all over our properties; and they have friends among those commissioners who decide where sidewalks should be placed. The long and short of this is, when you travel between the houses, use the bridal path.

"It's the same thing with your car. My aunts have no garage. A couple of centuries ago there was a carriage house; but it collapsed before I was born. If you parked your car down there, it would have to be in the street, and my home owner's insurance would not cover it. It would also contradict their belief that cars did not exist in the eighteenth century."

He gave a Wal-Mart bag that he had been holding to Carla. "This contains ordinary doll clothing. My wife had a great idea. She suspects that my aunts would love to dress the dog in doll's garments. She saw a regular baby carriage - I'm serious - it's for a real human child, and she thought they might benefit from putting the dog in it. A toy carriage is not stable. A real one is. Daphne could hold on as though it were a walker and Winifred could hold a kind of leash tied to the handle so that she could walk alongside it. Only about ten percent of her vision remains. Sybil pushed it down the bridal path to test how well it negotiated the uneven surface. She said it was fine. We ought to be coming to it soon."

As they reached the carriage, Roland opened the carrying box and handed the chihuahua pup to Carla. "They will melt when they see you bringing them this adorable creature." He began to push the carriage.

"I'm sure they will," she replied.

They entered the Buehler property through a wooden gate in a stone wall that was covered with ivy. The gate creaked as Roland pushed it open, and a spring mechanism slammed it shut behind them as they proceeded towards the house.

The aunts not only did not melt at the sight of them, but Daphne stood up in the kitchen as Roland opened the door. "We do not require much of you, Roland," she said in a chastising tone, "but we have asked that you announce yourself before coming here. And I see that you have brought a stranger. Am I to shrug my shoulders and say, 'Ah, he is too old to learn good manners,' and let this transgression pass?"

"Now, Aunt Daphne," Roland pleaded, "don't be too quick to object. I've brought you a lady who is a physician and a student at the University Medical School. We're having work done on her attic apartment in our house, so I asked her if she would be willing to stay here for a couple of days. I know that you would never put a lady out on the street. Besides, she has brought you a special gift."

"Thank you, Roland. Just leave the doggie carrying case and the pram there by the door and give the creature to Winifred." She turned to Carla. "Would you care for a cup of tea... Doctor?"

"Yes, I'd like that very much. My name is Carla Richards. Please call me Carla and let me apologize in advance if my presence here has disturbed you in any way."

Roland sniffed. "Well, I'm off. No good deed ever goes unpunished. Someday I may learn why I have incurred such enmity."

No one said a word until the garden gate had closed behind him.

"Please sit down, and tell us, Doctor Richards, how long you have lived with our nephew."

"Carla, please," she said, sitting at the kitchen table. "I arrived in Baltimore on the 2nd, interviewed for a house-sitter's position with him on the 4th, and moved into his home on the 5th."

"And already on the 13th he's moving you in with us? Have you been given any special instructions?" Daphne asked.

"None. Just to enjoy life here at the Buehler house and to be on hand if you should need me. I go to school. I'm taking medical refresher courses at the university."

The aunts proceeded to ask Carla about her background. By the time they finished their second cup of tea, Winifred was playing with the dog. "This poor creature has a deformed leg. Look, Daphne. She's shivering."

"I have some doll's clothes Mrs. Melbourne bought for her. I don't know if they fit, but maybe there's a coat in here." She handed her the bag.

There was a sweater among the miniature garments. Winifred put the sweater over the dog's head and managed to get her front legs through the arms. "What is her name?" she asked.

"That is for you to decide," Carla replied.

"Then I shall call her Bonbon... she's such a sweet little dessert caramel candy... all covered in milk chocolate."

Daphne placed a wicker peck basket upside down on the fourth chair at the table. Then she placed a folded towel on it to act as a cushion and placed Bonbon on top. She moved the chair in so that it really looked as though Bonbon was an ordinary guest at the kitchen table. The ladies laughed.

For an hour they seemed to be fully occupied with the dog, but in that time they elicited Carla's entire life story.

"Pinatubo. Such a disaster!" Daphne said. "We had a great aunt who loved to describe the sunsets after Krakatoa erupted. She told us that for two years afterwards, the whole world was treated to the most amazingly beautiful sunsets."

"Sunrises, too," Winifred added.

Finally it was decided that Carla should take her overnight bag up to the guest room. Carla followed their instructions and found herself in a colonial bedroom with a bed that seemed as short as a child's crib. As she looked around the room, the front door bell sounded. The caterer was delivering their dinners. Carla went to the top of the stairs and watched the caterer leave. Simultaneously, Roland knocked at the back door. He had brought Carla's dinner in an insulated container.

As Carla descended the stairs, Roland had already exited the kitchen. She heard Daphne say, "What can he be up to this time?"

"You'll have to watch him closely, Daphne."

As Carla sat at the table, she asked, "Have you heard whether they caught the man who was committing those home invasions?"

"What home invasions?" Daphne asked.

"Oh, just something I heard. Nothing to worry about."

"I do believe that we will require a little place setting for Mistress Bonbon," Winifred said. Daphne immediately went to the hutch cabinet and returned with a small pewter bowl.

"It looks old," Carla noted.

"Ah, we believe it dates to 1770," Daphne said, placing bits of filet mignon in the bowl. "Yes... we live steeped in history... we're like two old tea bags in a Ching Dynasty porcelain tea pot."

"They didn't have tea bags," Winifred corrected her sister.

"Then we're a couple of old strainers. They did have those."

All three women put food in Bonbon's bowl. "Did you know," Winifred asked, "that Queen Elizabeth the Second used to feed her corgis on sterling silver... and then someone made a fuss about it so she had to stop? Nobody could object to pewter... pewter is just tin and copper and a few other things."

Carla put the kettle on for after-dinner tea. She cleared the table and turned on the hot water in the sink to wash the flatware they had used. "I'll wash the utensils right away before any food dries on the tines." When she returned to the table, tea was being poured. A sterling silver bowl had replaced the pewter one.

Daphne said, "Why shouldn't Mistress Bonbon eat off sterling? That Queen Elizabeth the Second's father was a George... the Sixth, I believe. The good Lord knows we had enough trouble with George the Third. Thomas Jefferson listed 27 grievances against him. Did you know that? You must read the Declaration of Independence. Mr. Jefferson was a brilliant scholar."

In the evening, as everyone retired, Carla looked up the fashions that were worn in 1776 and found a country woman's jacket and petty coat and a straw hat that was secured by a ribbon around the chin. She also searched for designer dressmakers for small dogs and found a shop that was near the medical school. On Monday, she decided, she would visit the shop and see if she could obtain colonial style garments for Mistress Bonbon. The ladies, she knew, would adore the outfit.

She laughed to herself. "Now the two spinsters have become four."

But, speaking of spinsters, there was her own love-life to attend to. Dwight Ingram and his daughter Chloe had come to Baltimore specifically to visit her. Dwight, having paid for so much of her present circumstance, had a right to expect her to be cordial and accommodating. He and Chloe had arrived at 2 p.m. They expected Carla to meet them at the airport; when she did not appear they took the motel's shuttle. She called and agreed to meet them at 8 p.m. for dinner, and it was already 7 p.m. and she did not know if she would be violating the terms of her contract if she left the aunts alone and drove down to Baltimore or whether she had a right to keep this "social" obligation.

The aunts were having a disagreement about which of them Bonbon would sleep with. "Carla," Winifred called, "can you come in here and settle this for us?"

"I, too, have a problem," she said. She settled the dog-sleeping problem by saying that they should alternate nights having the dog sleep in their bedrooms. The aunts agreed to compromise. It was a good solution.

"And what is your problem?" Daphne asked.

Carla explained her troubling situation and then added, "I know Roland wants me to stay here because you're afraid of some burglar who's plaguing the neighborhood. But I made this appointment before I even met Roland. I don't know what to do."

"A lady keeps her promises - in the order that she made them," Winifred said definitively. "You better hurry and get dressed. It is Saturday night and the traffic may be more than you expect, going down to Baltimore. When you go to get your car, walk down the street. The bridal path is much too muddy and dangerous to travel on at night."

Carla thanked the aunts, got dressed for her date, and then defied Roland's commandment that she always use the bridal path, and walked down the street to get her car.

Dwight Ingram had begun to wonder why he had bothered to make the trip. He and Chloe had spent the entire afternoon watching television in a motel room. At 5 p.m. he had ordered a pizza.

Carla arrived at 8:20 p.m. Dwight asked, "Where would you like to eat?"

"I don't know any restaurants," she replied. "I had excellent seafood in one, but I don't remember where it was."

"Is that where George and Beryl took you?" Chloe asked.

"Yes. George and I also ate in the Student Union cafeteria."

"Come on," Dwight said. "We can ask the desk clerk where three semi-hungry folks can get a good meal."

The clerk listed the six top restaurants - none of which had an available reservation. They walked to the nearest Starbuck's and had lattees and muffins and talked pleasantly until the place closed at 10 p.m. When they left, Dwight held Carla's hand as Chloe conveniently announced that she had her own room at the motel and was looking forward to a snore-free night of sleep.

During their phone conversations, Dwight and Carla had spoken intimately to each other. Being together physically was mutually understood as the reason for their meeting in Baltimore.

When they returned to the motel, Carla wanted to get into her car and drive back to Dalton Creek; but she didn't. She had, in essence, promised this liaison, and the least she could do was to pretend that she welcomed it.

She did not park her car again outside the Melbourne residence until 7 a.m. Sunday morning.

SUNDAY, OCTOBER 14, 2012

"Did you have fun with your beau?" Winifred asked as they had breakfast tea together with Mistress Bonbon.

"Yes," Carla said. "It was nice to see him and his daughter again."

"Invite them to tea, my dear," Daphne said. "We adore company."

Carla checked the time. It was after nine o'clock. "All right, I'll call him." She called the motel. Dwight answered with a grunted, "Yes?" She did not know if his hoarse voice was due to annoyance or sleepiness. "I wanted to invite you to tea... up here in Dalton Creek."

"Where?"

"It's just north of town... some forty miles or so."

"I didn't bother to rent a car. The motel had shuttle service, and you said you'd be driving yours."

"It was just a thought. I had a wonderful time last night. Call me when you get the chance." She whispered, "Goodbye," and heard him grunt something and disconnect the call.

"I have so much studying to do," she explained to the aunts. "I guess it's just as well."

She went to her room and tried to study. For the first time since she arrived in Maryland she felt depressed, disappointed in herself, feeling used and, worse, feeling that she was a user. She fully expected Roland to come to the Buehler house to chastise her for leaving the aunts alone on Saturday night. "Well," she thought, "I've managed to alienate George and Dwight... why not Roland, too?"

Roland did not disappoint. At noon he appeared at the kitchen door and demanded to know why on a Saturday night - of all nights - she had elected to spend the evening away from her "post."

"She did no such thing!" Daphne snapped. "Winnie and I sent Carla down to Georgetown to lend the Giekie's a couple of serving dishes they needed to complete their set for a party. We wanted her to stay and retrieve the silver dishes and not depend on them to return them. God knows what we would have received in place of the originals. You should be thanking Carla, not criticizing her."

Roland mumbled an apology and left. He was not entirely convinced, but he reasoned that it was much too soon for Carla to have cultivated such a degree of loyalty that his aunt would lie for her.

MONDAY, OCTOBER 15, 2012

On Monday Carla picked up a colonial style dog dress that came with a petty coat and hat and brought it to the aunts.

Sitting at the dinner table, Mistress Bonbon wore colonial garb as she perched upon the basket and ate bits of meat that were placed on a sterling silver plate.

Owing to Aunt Winifred's eyesight, television was not a possibility for after-dinner entertainment. Since Daphne's voice was still hoarse from reading the Sunday newspaper to Winifred, Carla asked, "Would you like me to read a novel to you? One chapter per night?" The ladies enthusiastically agreed, and Carla went to a secretarial desk's bookshelf and selected *Moby Dick*.

She lit the fire in the parlor, and while the mistresses Daphne, Winifred, and Bonbon sat comfortably on the Duncan Phyfe couch, Carla sat beside a table on which two tall candles were lit, and began to read: "Chapter One," she said. *"Call me Ishmael..."*

Even Bonbon was silently enthralled as Carla read on to the concluding paragraph: *By reason of these things, then, the whaling voyage was welcome; the great flood-gates of the wonder-world swung open, and in the wild conceits that swayed me to my purpose, two and two there floated into my inmost soul, endless processions of the whale, and, mid most of them all, one grand hooded phantom, like a snow hill in the air.*

For a reason she did not understand, the image of a huge pale ghost looming over her horizon refused to leave her mind. She remembered the first time when she was doing a rotation in the coroner's laboratory and a body bag was laid on the pathologist's table and casually unzipped to reveal a maggot-filled corpse. For weeks after, she could not close her eyes without seeing the nauseating wriggle of a thousand white worms.

"Oh, do read another chapter," Winifred begged.

"No," Daphne said. "One chapter per night. Mistress Carla has to study her own school work. Tomorrow we will hear another chapter and the day after that, another one."

FRIDAY, OCTOBER 19, 2012

Since Fridays were usually only half a day at school, Carla drove north to Dalton Creek, intending to go shopping. She had called Chloe to apologize for having neglected her and her father during "that abysmal weekend," and Chloe responded by inviting Carla to come to Lake George, New York for Thanksgiving Dinner on November 22nd. In addition to the winter clothing she needed, she wanted to buy a nice cocktail dress for the occasion.

Roland called on her cellphone while she was still on the highway. "I'm glad I caught you in time," he said. "I have two important things I need to discuss with you. First, Daphne is overdue for her appointment with the orthopedic specialist. His secretary called, and I agreed to bring my dear aunt in for her check up. Winter is coming and when you've got bone problems, it is no fun. I'm hoping you'll accompany us to the doctor's office. Frankly it gets to be a bit awkward when I try to do it alone."

"Certainly, I'll go. What time is the appointment?"

"One o'clock. Why don't you just come inside when you park your car? I'll have Daphne here and we can go into town, and after her appointment, I've made another one to see a new Toyota for you. I spoke to a salesman and told him that you had job security and were obviously a responsible person. Even for a stripped down version, you'd have to make a substantial down payment. I'm willing to lend you $4000 and he'll let you finance the rest. So, what I'm thinking is that after we leave the doctor's office we can stop at the dealers and get your car problem squared away."

"That's wonderful, but how would I pay you back?"

"How does a hundred dollars a month sound? That would be on top of a relatively small car payment."

"Then I'd be thrilled to accept. I'd also like to do a little shopping after we bring Daphne home. Would that be a problem?"

"No, not at all. The doctor should take only an hour or so, the same with the dealer, and the stores are open late on Friday nights."

At 12:30 p.m. Carla parked outside the Melbourne's house and, as she walked around to the front door, discovered Roland waiting on the steps. "I'm glad we have a few minutes," he said. "I've got a lovely surprise in the solarium. A new orchid plant! I want to memorialize it."

Carla entered the house and was startled to see Daphne and Bonbon sitting in the living room.

"If we hurry," Roland said, "I can get a few pictures. The maid agreed to stay and take photographs of the four of us." He jovially ushered them into his solarium.

Half a dozen photographs of Carla holding the orchid, Daphne, and Roland holding Bonbon were taken; and then he handed the dog to the maid who walked back towards the kitchen as he hurried his aunt and Carla out of the house.

"But what about Bonbon?" Carla asked.

"She'll be fine," Roland assured her and Daphne, whose expression indicated that she did not want to be separated from the dog.

"Winifred will be worried," Daphne said.

"We won't be long," Roland assured her.

They drove into town and kept the doctor's appointment. Daphne apprehensively kept looking at her watch.

"We'll be home soon," Carla whispered. "Everything will be fine, but we do have one other stop to make."

At the Toyota dealer's showroom, Carla found that the paperwork, which included a promissory note, had already been mostly completed. Roland regretted that his employer frowned upon any of his key personnel co-signing anybody's notes - not friends and not family. He produced $4000 in cash and Carla signed many documents and was permitted to drive the new Toyota from the lot.

Daphne had remained in Roland's car. As they drove, with Carla following, Roland received a phone call. He said a few words and then proceeded to drive directly to the aunts' house. "All right, Ladies," he said. "I have a minor emergency to attend to." He helped Daphne get out of the car.

Winifred had been waiting near the front door and as soon as she heard the car pull up she opened the door.

While Carla parked and then went to attend to Daphne, Roland, without another word, drove away.

"Where is Bonbon?" Winifred called, crying.

"I'll go down to Roland's and get her," Carla said and began to jog down the street to the Melbourne's house.

She unlocked the front door, punched the security system keypad, and called for Bonbon. A whimpering sound came from behind the cellar door. Carla tried the door which was securely locked. She recalled that she had not seen the maid's car out front and realized that no one was home.

She tried to comfort the dog as she called Roland's cellphone, asking for an immediate call back. Bonbon had been left locked in the cellar and she didn't know where the key to the cellar door was. After fifteen minutes, she called Sybil's cellphone and also had to leave a message. She waited another distressing fifteen minutes of trying to comfort the frightened animal and then she decided that the best thing to do was to drive Beryl's car to the Buehler house to get Winifred. It would comfort both her and the dog, even if they were on either side of a locked door.

Two hours later, Roland returned, apologetic that his emergency made him forget all about the dog. "The maid simply shouldn't have left her alone," he said, unlocking the door.

Winifred, tightlipped, stared at Roland until the door was opened and the dog jumped into her arms to kiss her face. She soothed it with promises that she would never be left alone again.

The aunts were so distraught by the events of the day that Carla postponed shopping for winter clothing until the next weekend. Roland, however, had other plans for the remainder of Carla's afternoon. He followed her up to Philadelphia so that she could drop Beryl's car off at the address George had given her.

Carla rode back to Dalton Creek with Roland and managed to say only a weak, "Thanks for all your help, today," as they drove back.

Sybil had brought Carla's dinner to the Buehler house and the aunts had kept it warm for Carla.

Daphne lit the fire in the parlor, and though Carla was emotionally exhausted, she nevertheless read Chapter 5 of *Moby Dick*.

As she lay in bed that night, it suddenly occurred to her that the maid had to have a key to the basement. Why, she wondered, was the basement off limits to her - the official house protector - but was accessible to the maid?

There were also used cars at the dealership. Why was it so important that she get a new one? Perhaps, she thought, in consideration of Roland's generosity, they did not want an old car parked so permanently in front of their home.

FRIDAY, OCTOBER 26, 2012

Carla left the Buehler house in the morning, saying that she did not have school that afternoon and would be home early. The weather was turning cold and she still owned no winter clothing and could no longer delay purchasing a coat and boots to wear in the snow.

When she walked down the bridal path to get her new car at the Melbourne's house, she decided to stop at the house and discuss Roland's plans for her future. She had been expected to stay at the Buehler's for only a couple of days. But several weeks had passed, and, while she was happy to live with the aunts, there were too many inconveniences to accommodate a long term residence with them. What, exactly, did he have in mind?

She went to the garage and saw that only Roland's car was still there. Sybil had obviously left for work and the maid had not yet arrived. Carla found the front door closed, but not locked - and the alarm system disarmed.

She walked through the living room and noticed that the cellar door was ajar. Without saying a word, she pulled the door open and descended the stairs. She found a large kitchen supply closet and two rows of files. One contained the records of the Buehler sisters and the other the records of the Melbournes. She opened a drawer that indicated that it contained current files and discovered that Roland worked for a company called "Advanced Alliance Associates." The name gave no clue regarding the nature of the company. She turned and ascended the stairs and left the door in the same position in which she had found it.

As she went up to her attic room, Roland, who was also getting ready to leave for work, came out of his bedroom and asked, "Will you go back to the Buehler house before you go shopping?"

She thought it was an odd question, but she answered, "Yes. I'll have lunch with them. I told them that if they thought of anything they needed at the department store, they should write it down and I'd get their list then."

"That was thoughtful of you," Roland said. He made no other comment as he left the house.

At noon, Carla returned from school, parked her car at the Melbourne house and walked down to the aunts' house to make sandwiches and tea for lunch. It had rained and Carla noticed that Daphne's coat was wet. The sisters seemed to be distracted. They whispered in the kitchen and when Carla entered the room, they pointedly stopped talking. "Is everything all right?" Carla asked.

"We are not 'sunshine patriots'" Daphne said sternly. "When called to take up arms, we must obey."

Carla did not understand the comment. Winifred tried to amplify the remark. "Sometimes, my dear, a snake says, 'Don't tread on me!' and if you do, you will regret it."

Carla still did not understand and smiled dumbly. Daphne said, "Perhaps King Lear said it best. 'How sharper than a serpent's tooth it is to have a thankless child.' Let us say no more about it."

A yellow manila envelope protruded from the pocket of the wet coat. Carla could read the source of the envelope: *MacEvoy and Morton, Attorneys at Law.* "Uh, oh," Carla thought, "maybe Daphne has finally gone to see an attorney about Roland."

As she served ice cream for dessert, the mood in the kitchen changed. Bonbon licked her little doggie cookie that was topped with vanilla ice cream. Her antics were, as usual, adorable as she again proved herself to be the most wonderful young lady in the Colonies.

Carla cleared the table and returned to Roland's house to get her car to go shopping.

At the Buehler house, it was time to take Bonbon out into the back lawn for her to do her part in keeping the shrubbery fertilized. Daphne always carried a small pail of potting soil and a garden rake to move the fertilizer-stub under a rhododendron bush and cover it with potting soil.

The front door bell of the Buehler house rang. "It's probably Carla," said Daphne. "Maybe she forgot something." She entered the kitchen, intending to walk through the house to open the front door. She noticed that the cellar door was ajar and as she extended her hand to close it, an arm reached out and grabbed her arm pulling her forward with a violent jerk, while a second arm struck her in the diaphragm, knocking the wind out of her so that she could not scream. The hooded figure that had attacked her wore a Halloween devil's mask. It was the last thing she saw as she was picked up and dumped down onto the flight of stairs.

After a minute or two, both Bonbon and Winifred had begun to shiver. Winifred made her way back into the house, entered the kitchen, and walked through to the living room. She sat on her rocking chair, listening for word from Daphne. She heard a noise coming unaccountably from the kitchen she had just passed through, and she called, "Daphne... is that you?"

Daphne did not answer. Instead, Winifred clearly heard the back door open and close. She perceived no threat and made herself comfortable, holding the dog against her chest, and humming a lullaby as the chair pitched gently back and forth, squeaking in a comforting cadence. Her nearly blind eyes closed as Bonbon, too, began to snooze in the time-captured freedom of the New World.

Carla returned from shopping to discover the house virtually surrounded by police cars, county vehicles, and a coroner's van.

Daphne had had a fatal accident. She had fallen down the cellar stairs. A forensic examiner had taken samples of flesh and her wool stockings that were on the top steps.

Carla immediately went to Winifred who ceaselessly rocked, holding Bonbon. "Brave Daphne!" was all she inexplicably would say.

FRIDAY, NOVEMBER 2, 2012

There no longer was a question about where Carla would reside. Winifred was alone.

Roland had made all the funeral arrangements and had personally escorted his aunt to Daphne's service. After the services, as he stood and talked to the few guests who attended, he assured their friends and neighbors that he wanted Winifred to come to his house to live - where he, his wife, and Carla would be there to care for her. "But," he lamented, "the dear lady is so obstinate and refuses to leave her house."

Carla had gone to the funeral services with Sybil and Barry, whom she met for the first time. She quickly formed the opinion that Barry was high. His eyes darted around, his hands moved pointlessly, and his nostrils showed unmistakable signs of irritation. He was also arrogant and seemed reluctant to speak to his aunt. His yellow Mustang stood out in the funeral procession to the cemetery, but during the reading of the graveside prayers, he quietly drifted back from the mourners and drove the yellow car away. He was not at home when his parents and aunt returned from the cemetery.

During the next few days, Roland acted as host as a few neighbors came to pay condolence calls on Winifred. Charles Merriweather asked if she would like him to oversee the donations of some of their antique furniture to the museums of her choice. She declined, saying, "I will have my attorney see to that."

Carla, as expected, was not invited to the reading of Daphne's will, but, she immediately realized, after seeing Roland and Sybil's response as they returned from the reading, that it had not gone the way they had expected. Daphne had changed her will and left everything she owned to Winifred - with the exception of an odd assortment of antiques which she left to Roland.

The odd assortment, Carla learned from her "impromptu" party friend Frances, were copies of antiques that Daphne suspected Roland and Barry of having already stolen.

Carla approached Roland to ask if more sensible adjustments could be made to her living arrangements. She would clear a space to park her car beside the Buehler house; their laundress now could do her laundry in place of Daphne's; and the caterer could still continue to deliver two meals to the aunts' house. She would simply eat the one that Daphne had previously eaten. "It would save you the trip of walking down with my dinner," she said enthusiastically.

Roland was shocked. "Is this the time to ask me about domestic issues? Can you not see that I am in mourning?"

SATURDAY, NOVEMBER 10, 2012

Roland called Carla on her cellphone and asked her to return quietly to his house for an important issue. He met her at the junction of the footpath and the tree line. He apologized for his previous rudeness and, recovering his poise, announced, "I have something more encouraging to tell you about." As they walked to his house, he confided, "I've received a call from the Smithsonian Museum. Aunt Daphne had promised them the gift of a few pieces of antique furniture." He showed Carla the copy of a letter that purported to be signed by Daphne. "Say nothing about this to Aunt Winifred. She's not quite herself these days, and I definitely do not want her distressed about anything. Anything at all! She needs to be cheered up, not entangled in arguments with museum curators."

"Won't she miss the pieces?"

"It is the custom of the museum to have copies of the antiques made so that the donor will not be plagued by the empty space and then, perhaps, regret having made the donation. A copy of the original will be supplied at the time the piece is picked up."

"I've been meaning to ask you if you would mind if I took Aunt Winifred to the Symphony tonight? She's expressed a fondness for Chopin and they're doing 'An Evening With Chopin.' I think it will cheer her up considerably."

"That's a wonderful idea!" Roland exclaimed. "Consider this month's loan payment to be paid in full by this wonderful gesture. By all means, take her to the concert!"

Carla was getting seriously behind in her studies and had wanted to spend Saturday night in her room trying to catch up with her classwork. But she had begun to feel a genuine affection for Winifred and was determined to lift her from her sorrowful mood. They went to the concert.

Winifred was thrilled. When the *Polonaise* was played, she murmured, "This is for brave Daphne."

On Sunday morning, Roland came by to take Winifred and Bonbon to the small dog park so that Bonbon could play safely with other small dogs. While they were gone, a black, step-in van came to the house and removed two pieces of furniture and delivered two others to replace them. Carla signed the receipt and gave her copy of it to Roland.

The following week Carla purchased two tickets to the Philadelphia Orchestra's "Evening of Beethoven and Wagner." She drove directly to the home of Betty-Lou Pemberton, an old schoolmate of Winifred's, and stayed in the Pemberton home in Bryn Mawr over Friday night. Bonbon did not object.

Once again, Winifred was thrilled with the music. Siegfried's Funeral March brought tears to her eyes; and Carla knew that she was thinking of "brave Daphne." But why "brave"? Carla did not dare to ask, although she did suspect that Roland had something to do with the accidental death.

Mistress Bonbon had spent the evening with Ms. Pemberton who assured the two theater-goers that the young lady had conducted herself with the decorum befitting her rank.

While Carla went to bed, the two old classmates stayed up for two hours talking quietly between themselves. Carla noticed that Winifred did not come to bed until 2 a.m.

They returned to Dalton Creek Saturday afternoon and again, on Sunday morning, as Roland took his aunt and the dog to the small dog park, the black van came again and removed more pieces of furniture and delivered their replacements.

On Sunday afternoon, however, Roland expressed his anger that Carla had risked his dear aunt's life by taking her so far away. Carla reminded him that she was a physician and that Winifred had never been in any danger at all. Winifred overheard the argument but said nothing.

Once again, on Sunday morning, the 18th of November, the black van came again to receive and to deliver furniture. Carla, as usual, signed the receipt and gave it to Roland.

It often happens that in an emotionally stressful time, the person who is suffering will find a source of help... a drink, a sleeping pill, a medication to reduce anxiety or depression, an aberrant behavior that provides a diverting excitement to the feelings of dread... only to discover that after the original crisis is past, the help that was employed to ease the stress has itself become a stressful malady for which the person requires help.

Carla Richards was supposed to be the antidote to the romantic poison given George by the other woman in his life, Lilyanne Smith, who was due to deliver her first child, a son, who was not, unfortunately, related to George. Now, needing an antidote for Carla, he sought to find it by keeping a stricter attendance to temple services and by adding a second night of playing shuffleboard with Sensei (now "abbot" of the little Zen temple) at their favorite pub.

He also sought to limit his toxic exposure by declining to return the few phone calls that Carla finally made to him. He missed her, and it hurt him to recall how much he had enjoyed being with her in the Philippines - a loving time that he had regarded as "soul-saving." He knew that if she confronted him directly, he would yield; and his pride was just a little too bruised to risk direct contact.

George completed his self-imposed exile from his own social life by announcing, before anyone had a chance not to invite him to dinner, that he would be spending the Thanksgiving Day holiday with his brother in Florida. They would be going fishing "for marlin probably." His brother was suffering from carpal tunnel syndrome and the last thing he was capable of doing was fishing for marlin, but George had underestimated the physical limitations of the condition.

Nevertheless, while Carla flew to Lake George to have holiday dinner with the Ingrams, George flew south and ate at least ten thousand calories a day at his brother's house and did nothing more physically demanding than pulling his suitcase off the airport carousel. (He had brought his new fishing gear with him.)

FRIDAY, NOVEMBER 23, 2012

Carla returned from Lake George, wishing that she had never gone. Travel foul-ups and other unfortunate misalignments had ruined what she had expected would be a festive relief from the troubling days in Maryland. She claimed her car at the airport and drove to the Melbourne's house. Winifred Buehler, as was the tradition, had eaten Thanksgiving Dinner with her nephew and had spent Thursday night in his guest room since Carla was not there to accompany her home. But on Friday morning, when, under Barry's watchful eye, Winifred took Bonbon out for her "morning relief," the little dog had panicked and run off; and Barry, given the choice of pursuing the dog or tending to his nearly blind aunt, chose, naturally, the latter.

In fact, Barry had stolen the dog intending to sell it to pay off a $1000 debt to his cocaine supplier. The product that had been given to Barry on consignment to sell to his college friends had inadvertently been consumed without payment; and the dealer was not inclined to be forgiving. Bonbon had been shoved into the Mustang's trunk compartment and was not in evidence when Roland and Sybil searched the area for the dog. Barry regretted that he had an early appointment with friends and drove away shortly after the dog had disappeared.

Carla arrived to find a tight-lipped Winifred who said only, "Carla, would you be kind enough to take me home immediately and then, on the outside chance that Mistress Bonbon really did run away, to search the nearby woods for her?"

Carla went along the bridal path repeatedly calling Bonbon's name, but the dog was not anywhere near the sound of her voice. When she returned to the Buehler house, Winifred asked if she would take her in one of Daphne's old canvas wheelchairs to neighboring streets so that they could call for Bonbon there. Carla complied, and to her surprise, while they were going down one of the adjacent streets, a limousine pulled up. The chauffeur got out and assisted Winifred as she got into the rear seat. "Tell no one where I am," she told Carla. "There is a coffee shop in the next block. Wait for me there. I will be back within the hour."

Carla went to the coffee house, collapsed the wheelchair and put it behind a bush, and then went in to sit over coffee and a muffin and to wonder why everything around her seemed to be spinning out of control. At one o'clock the limo pulled up to the curb. As Winifred was helped from the vehicle, Carla left the shop and set up the wheel chair to push the sorrowful aunt back to her home.

Roland, too, insisted on helping to find the dog. He designed a "Reward For Missing Dog" flyer. "Tomorrow morning," he asked Carla, "would you be kind enough to take this into town and have a few hundred copies run off so that I can take them around to businesses and telephone poles? And also, would you stop at the animal shelter to see if our precious little girl has been rescued by them?"

Carla agreed to go. But there was still an evening to be spent without Bonbon. Because Winifred had believed that Daphne's spirit was still present with them and that she enjoyed the nightly reading of *Moby Dick*, Carla had continued to read the book, sometimes reading two chapters on any night that she expected to be unavailable for the following night's reading. "A promise," Winifred insisted, "was a promise." That night Chapter 40 of *Moby Dick* was due to be read.

Carla lit the fire and Winifred, rocking with the deliberation of a Madame Defarge, listened as Carla read the chapter. When she read the concluding lines: *"Oh, thou big white God aloft there somewhere in yon darkness, have mercy on this small black boy down here; preserve him from all men that have no bowels to feel fear!"* A grim smile crossed her lips and she said, "Good night, my dear," as she got up from her rocking chair and made her way slowly to the staircase.

SATURDAY, NOVEMBER 24, 2012

Soon after Carla left to go to the Animal Shelter to search for Bonbon, Winifred, too, had a fatal accident on the cellar stairs. But this time, there was no tissue or fabric caught on the upper steps, and it appeared as if she had indeed been propelled down the stairs. According to the medical examiner, she had landed on her chest and face on the lower steps. Carla returned from the Animal Shelter to find the house, once again, surrounded by official vehicles. But this time, she was taken in for questioning.

It was then that she learned that Roland had insisted that she had never lived with the aunts and had gone there only occasionally to check on them. While he was looking through his aunt's things, he discovered receipts for valuable antiques that Carla had signed. He had no idea where she put the money she received for them. Yes, they were all insured; but money could not replace such precious items of Americana. What a terrible thing it was to be deceived by a foreigner who had no respect for the country he, or she, was taking advantage of.

After six hours of questioning, Carla was exhausted. Roland came to the police station and demanded that she surrender the keys to his home and any keys that she had made to the Buehler house. He asked that a deputy be present while Carla gathered her things from his home. Accompanied by the police officer, she returned to the Melbourne house, packed her clothing, books, and toiletries in boxes, accepted a plastic bag of soiled garments that the maid had not yet had the chance to launder, and was escorted from the premises as Roland reminded her of the terms of the confidentiality agreement which was still in effect and also of her note which she was still obliged to pay. She returned to Baltimore and asked a schoolmate if she could possibly share a room until she could get situated.

She wanted to call George, but she feared the repercussions that would ensue if she violated the confidentiality agreement. She was also embarrassed by her attitude towards him when he had offered to investigate the job opportunity.

Once again, the Melbournes were stunned to learn of irrevocable changes Winifred had made to her will.

As Attorney Gerald Morton would later assert, "The lady's mind was clear. She was neither morose nor euphoric. She had no complaints to register against anyone. She merely claimed that since her sister's death, she had revived an old passion for classical music and wanted to establish scholarship funds for young musicians at several music schools, and also, as a victim, herself, of Retinitis pigmentosa, she wanted money to be donated to several research facilities in the attempt to find a cure for this affliction. She entrusted the disposition of these funds to Doctor Carla Richards, a citizen of the Philippines who currently was studying medicine in Maryland. She provided the sum of one thousand dollars each to Roland, Sybil, and Barry, and made provisions for the care of the chihuahua dog that she called Bonbon, and that, if at all possible, the dog be laid to rest with her and her sister whenever the animal passed on."

It was due to Gerald Morton's report to the District Attorney that both Winifred and Daphne had expressed fear and suspicion of the Melbournes that Carla Richards was not immediately investigated and required to give her passport to the authorities. Despite Roland Melbourne's clamoring for Carla's arrest, the District Attorney was not inclined to arrest her, "at the moment." It also stood in Carla's favor that Barrington Melbourne was well known to the police in Dalton Creek, Baltimore, and Hagerstown as a drug user.

SATURDAY, DECEMBER 8, 2012

In such dismal prospects did George spend the succeeding weeks after Thanksgiving, that on the December day that he, Beryl, and Sensei received invitations to attend the December 8th Christening of Lilyanne's baby boy, he made reservations for a flight to California to visit his teenaged kids, a visit that, "as luck would have it," would occur while the Christening ceremony was being held.

On the five-hour flight across country he considered female toxicity. Poison #1, his ex-wife; Poison #2, Lilyanne Smith; and Poison #3, Carla Richards, M.D. "Some men are born to live bitterly alone," he told himself, "and I am one of them."

On the Saturday morning of the Christening, George was helping his son to master Euler's Formulas in trigonometry in preparation for his college entrance exam, while his daughter, a solid A in mathematics, went shopping for new boots.

George felt a pang of schadenfreude on Saturday evening when Sensei called to complain that more days had passed without his having heard from the love of *his* life, the exquisite Sonya Lee of Hong Kong. "It's just not like her to stay out of touch with me for three straight months," he complained.

"Ah," George said, "she's an important agent. She's probably on assignment. She gets some tough cases."

"Misery," George repeated to himself, "loves company." Then he chastised himself for feeling even slight relief that he was not alone in his romantic despair.

He would never have expected that on his return to Philadelphia, he would find Carla Richards sitting in his office, begging him for his help to acquit her of charges she believed were soon going to be filed against her: twenty-seven counts of grand larceny and at least one count of murder.

It was an awkward Christening. Lilyanne Smith was not married yet she named her son, Eric Tarleton Haffner, after the baby's father. She had substituted her mother's maiden name for the father's middle name which she did not happen to know.

The priest who officiated assumed that she surely had a husband who, if still alive, must be in military service; and he did not pry into the father's absence. There were no paternal grandparents present and he felt that as long as he was dispelling so much doubt, he might let his questions about them vaporize as well. He therefore assumed that they, if still alive, must be non-Catholics.

The moral persuasion of wealth and refinement quickly swept away all of the priest's residual curiosity. Felice and James Barton, Lilyanne's cousins, whom he did know, were the godparents of baby Eric. Additionally, there was a six-figure donation to the church; a well-known professional photographer; $2,000 worth of ribboned white orchids for the altar and baptismal chapel; and the music of Vivaldi which the organist had been handsomely paid to play.

Lilyanne Smith, twenty pounds heavier than she had been when she conceived young Eric, looked both radiant and regal in a yellow lace gown. She happily posed with her son during the ceremony in the church and afterwards during the reception in her home, Tarleton House. She asked Beryl Tilson to use her iPhone to take extra photographs of her alone and of her with the baby, and then she called Beryl aside. "As soon as there's a break in the action, can you meet me back in the greenhouse where we can talk privately?"

Half an hour later, there was such a break and the two women walked back through the snow to the glass building. "How is George?" Lily asked. "Is he still mad at me?"

"He was never mad. He was hurt."

"Weren't you ever able to tell him the truth?"

"You know George. He refused to discuss it."

"I know he wouldn't listen to me when I tried to tell him that he had gotten it all wrong, but I figured by now you'd be able to get through to him."

"No. Not me and not Sensei. Last March, when George got home from the Cayman Islands, he sat us down in his office and said that if we so much as mentioned your name to him or tried, in any way, to interject ourselves into what he called, 'The Cayman Islands Affair,' he would dissolve the partnership and that would be the end of Wagner and Tilson, Private Investigators, and also his membership in our Zen Buddhist sangha. He also told Sensei that if he so much as mentioned you, he would never again play shuffleboard with him at the Two Kegs Tavern or anyplace else… which was probably a more meaningful threat than resignation from the sangha. Lilyanne, he meant it. Your name, as the CIA would say, was 'terminated with extreme prejudice.'"

"Is he still alone in his house?"

"He had a new gal in his life… Carla, a doctor from the Philippines… but that seems to be dying away, too. So, yes, he's still alone. When it comes to romance, George retreats. That's how he deals with emotional problems. He's like a tortoise with an eggshell carapace."

"Well, I love him and I'll always love him and he knows that. So let him be as obstinate as he wants to be. I know that he loves me, and when he's ready, he'll come around. Meanwhile, I want to ask you for three favors."

"Sure, anything."

Lily pointed to a photo machine. "I had the servants bring this back here. It can print out glossy or matte finished copies of digital photographs. I want to pick a couple of the ones you took of me alone and of me and the baby. Just print them out for me… a couple of copies each."

Beryl looked through the photographs and with Lilyanne's approval selected two to be printed.

"The second favor is advice. What should I do about Eric and his parents? I know that as a civilized person I'm supposed to at least give them the information that they have a grandson. I don't want to start anything with Eric down in the Caymans. He's crazy enough to sneak up here and do anything from killing me, to kidnapping the baby, to moving into my bedroom and daring me to have him evicted - under penalty of a scandal. But his parents? Somehow I think they ought to be told. What do you think?"

"Well... let's see," Beryl said thoughtfully. "We've got a State Department and your father has a lot of drag with diplomats. So why not select one particularly nice photograph of yourself with the baby, maybe at the baptismal font and another of the baby alone - use the ones taken by the professional photographer - and send them to your dad's contact in the consul's office in Vienna. Ask him to present the photographs and a copy of the Christening announcement to Mr. and Mrs. Haffner. Let him explain that you're quite rich enough, thank you very much, and neither need nor want their money, and that simple civility prompts you to advise them of the existence of their grandchild. No further communication is necessary unless they feel that they'd like to meet the child for themselves, in which case, the good offices of the consul can be employed to arrange a meeting at some future time. Tell the consul that if they ask for your address, he should give it to them."

"Excellent!" said Lilyanne. "I knew you'd be the one who'd give me sensible advice. Can you come by when the photographs are done and help me to pick the best ones?"

"Sure. Is that the third favor?"

"No." Lilyanne reached into the neckline of the dress she was wearing and pulled out a gold chain on which was suspended the brass key to George Wagner's front door that he had once given her. Letting the key be a very visible pectoral pendant, she went down an aisle of the hothouse and found a blooming Monja Blanca orchid which she cut and placed over her ear. "Would you take my photograph and also print it?"

Beryl knew where this photograph would be sent, but she knew also that if Lilyanne managed to sneak it into George's view, he would want to see it however much he objected to its presence. She took half a dozen photographs until she got one that she thought was particularly beautiful. She printed several copies of it and the two women returned to the reception.

MONDAY, DECEMBER 17, 2012

George regretted that he had not parked his pickup inside the garage when he returned from California the previous evening. A neighbor's boy had left his skateboard propped up against George's garage door, and George hadn't wanted the hassle of getting out of the pickup to move it. It was still there, but overnight, it snowed; and now, as he stood in his little-used front doorway, his breath blew clouds around his nose and mouth and his shoulders flexed and relaxed and he spanked his hands together and prepared to step through the snow to get into the pickup's frozen seat. He was still breathing clouds inside the truck as he waited for the heater and defrosters to do their jobs, when he looked around and decided he loved the look of the street, especially when it wore the raiment of new-fallen snow.

It was early, and the morning sun had not risen high enough to tatter purity's garment. All the sharp and ugly angles were delicately curved. He wished that the soft white blanket would remain intact, but people would come and, just as he looked down to see his trail of footprints in the snow, they'd also disturb the loveliness with their presence. He thought of Sartre: *Hell is other people.* He smiled and released the emergency brake.

By the time he reached his office and parked in the rear, many cars were on the street and the business day had begun in earnest. An unfamiliar car with Maryland plates was parked beside his reserved space. Wondering whether the car's presence would bring good or bad news, he entered the office through the rear door and tried to act surprised to find Carla Richards sitting in conversation with Beryl.

"What's up, Ladies?" he said, affecting a casual greeting. Carla was too worried to respond in kind.

Beryl, hearing the office door open, got up from his desk. "I'll leave you three to talk about the problem." Akara had come to the office specifically to sit in on George's discussion with Carla.

George called them back into the kitchen. "While you tell me what's on your mind, I'll make–" he paused to look at Carla as if she were a friendly stranger, "whatever you prefer. Coffee or tea?"

"Tea. I'm in trouble, George," Carla said. "And I don't understand how or why."

"Hmm. What kind of trouble?" He kept his eyes on the tea canister. She began to cry. "I don't know where to begin."

"Again..." he said, trying and failing to sound professional, "what is the nature of the trouble? Cut off the wrong leg? Flunk out of school? Get charged with a crime?"

Carla looked up at him. "All right! All right! I should have listened to you! You were right and I was wrong!" She took a deep breath. "I haven't been officially charged with a crime but I think I will be soon." Again, she cried.

"Charged with what? Look, Carla, I can't help you if I don't know what the hell is wrong," he said curtly. "So try to focus on the problem and start at the beginning." There would be no mistaking his help for an effort to ingratiate himself with her... not this time!

"I'm sorry if I'm not being informative. I'm just so confused. Roland Melbourne - the man whose house I moved into - is a crook, and I walked right into his scheme."

"What are you going to be charged with?" Akara asked as he sat down at the table.

"Twenty-seven counts of larceny and probably the murder of one or both of the aunts."

"Oh," George replied, using a tone that could have indicated, "Is that all?" But he quickly corrected the tone and said, "Murder and theft. What does he say you stole from him?"

Carla sat at the little table and held her fingers against her forehead. "Not from him. From his elderly aunts. They had a house filled with really valuable antiques."

"Oh," George said in the attitude of a wise old owl. "This is an old story. But let's hear your version of it. Start from the moment you moved into your dream position."

Carla shuddered and wiped her eyes. "For the first week everything was fine. Roland gave an impromptu party and I got to meet the neighbors and a few associates from his office. He took time off from work to go with me to Motor Vehicles to help me to get my Maryland driver's license. He took me to the bank so that I could open an account. He was wonderful. Everything seemed perfect."

"Wonderful?" George shook his head. "He was officially establishing your residence in his house."

"How did you know that?" She was surprised that he had seen so clearly what she was only beginning to suspect.

"Please... don't waste time questioning me. Go on with the story. Where was the aunts' house?"

"Less than half a kilometer down the road. It's a colonial neighborhood." Her voice trailed off into a shuddering sob.

"And then?" George's tone noticeably softened. "How did you get involved with the aunts?"

"After I was there at Roland's house for a week, he told me that things were not quite right with the two aunts, Winifred and Daphne Buehler. Do you remember? I told you that he had said I'd have to look in on them from time to time. So he took me down to meet them."

"Yes. I remember. Why weren't they invited to your 'impromptu' party?"

"The older one had Retinitis pigmentosa - she was nearly blind. The younger one had severe osteoarthritis. She sometimes used a wheelchair, but she was able to get around with a cane. He said that he recently had them at the house for dinner. Both of them were born in August so it was a family tradition for them to have a big dinner at his house before his son went away to school. They also had Thanksgiving Day dinner and Christmas and Easter dinner at his house, too."

"Yes. And when other people were present, the aunts were not invited."

"Why should that make a difference?"

"Because he was keeping you separate from them in the public's eye."

"But why? I don't understand why he would do that."

"Because he's a thief and a thief needs to shift the blame onto somebody else! He had to make a villain of you... a sneak thief. You saw a quick way to make a buck and you took it. You were supposed to be working for him and instead you sneaked down to the aunts' house and started to steal from them.

"If you, as a stranger, moved into their house, the first time something disappeared you'd be blamed and fired. He had to keep you in their house as their friend, someone who was above suspicion. He probably knew that they already suspected him and he needed to be able to continue to steal. Nobody can steal a houseful of antiques at once - not with two living women in it. Naturally, he had to give you access to their house and its contents. You were set up. But wait a minute..." George wore the expression of omniscient weariness. "You said, 'Was.' Two months ago they were alive and well. Now they're in the past tense? So when did things start to go wrong?"

"After a week in Roland's house, he said some crisis had come up and I'd have to live with the aunts for a few days. There had been a home invasion in the neighborhood, and it had upset the aunts. He explained how much he cared about them and gave me some private family history.

"He told me there had been an old family feud that was exacerbated by their age. His mother should have gotten a third of the grandparents' estate, but she was left out of the will because she had married his father who was a poor but honorable man. He loved his aunts, he said. They helped him out when he needed help. So he was happy to do all kinds of work for them... took them to their doctor's visits, oversaw the repairs and maintenance of their house and grounds, paid their taxes, and handled their financial affairs including payment of their domestic bills and employees - the gardener and cleaning lady. He added that their attorney kept a watchful eye on everything he did for them. I had seen their financial records in his basement.

"He wanted me to guard the ladies so I said, 'fine' and carried down my books and clothes. Their house doesn't have a garage so I left my car at Roland's house, parked at the side of the two-car garage's driveway. The funny thing was that it was Roland who told the aunts about the home invasion, and they didn't seem all that worried about it."

"Wasn't it on the TV news or in the newspapers?"

"I didn't know anything about it; but then, I don't keep up with the local news. One street is the same as any other when you don't know the names of any of them. But at their house, Daphne usually read the morning paper to Winifred. I supposed that she had overlooked it."

"The home invasion story had no other purpose but to get you to live secretly in the house. What was that bullshit story he gave you about needing a person in residence, 'as a deterrent to crime,' I think is how you put it?"

"When I went for the interview, he told me about his son Barry's wild friends. He didn't want to leave the house unattended for fear that they'd come in and cause all kinds of trouble. But he didn't want Barry to know he was putting a guard in the tower, watching him, so to speak. So I was the deterrent to his friends."

"Why didn't you mention that when you talked to me? Did he hold you to secrecy?"

"Yes. And like a fool I believed what he said. What's worse is that I found prescriptions for cocaine withdrawal medications in Barry's room... and not only that but I signed a confidentiality agreement."

"Good Christ!" He still did not feel like being charitable. "Well, nobody forced you to sign it. Is it a mutual agreement for confidentiality... or are you the only one who is bound not to talk?"

"It's just me." She produced the contract.

George looked at it. "You've even agreed to keep the contract confidential."

"I know. I was a fool. Have you never done anything that you regretted?"

George sighed. "Many things." His attitude changed. "Meeting you is not one of them. All right. You do realize that if I am engaged to help you and I have a financial incentive for giving you that help, I am soliciting you to break a contract for my own personal benefit. I could easily be included in a suit against you." Carla groaned and, still crying, tried to get up from the table. George grabbed her and held her while her body convulsed in sobs. "It's all right," he whispered. "I'm not afraid of twerps like him. You did the right thing in coming to us. What were these antiques and furniture pieces that you're alleged to have stolen?" He helped her to sit down again at the table.

"Chests, cabinets, bedroom furniture... and all kinds of colonial things... bellows... dishes... pewter... sterling flatware." She related the circumstances of Daphne and Winifred's death.

"What ruse did he use to blame you for stealing the furniture?"

"After Daphne died he told me that she had promised several museums that she'd give them some antiques. He wanted to get Winifred some exercise and keep her from becoming despondent over Daphne's death, so on Sunday mornings he took her and the aunts' chihuahua Bonbon to the small dog park."

"And a van came and took a few antiques and replaced them with cheap antiques and you accepted delivery of the fakes..."

"Oh, God. Yes. That's what happened."

"Don't worry. I'm not going to say, 'I told you so.' And the possible murder charges? Probably he first had to get rid of the aunt who could see. Which one was she?"

"Daphne. On October 26th."

"Where were you when the accident occurred?"

"I had gone shopping. It was a Friday afternoon. I had a lot to get done. Things to buy. I had just moved here from Luzon, George! I needed cold weather clothing. The coroner said she had been dead several hours... but her frailty and the damp cold of the basement could have influenced the time."

"Did they investigate further?"

"Yes, the police determined from the scrapes on her knees and the heel of her hand and from the tissue left on the edge of the top steps that she hadn't been propelled... not pushed... down the stairs. She had just fallen forward while she was reaching for something on one of the shelves they had built in the stairwell.

"But on November 24th, Winifred also fell down the same stairs and her fall was not so clearly accidental," Carla said, her speech quickening. "Daphne wore culottes because of the comfort and convenience. And she wore woolen stockings because of her arthritis. There was skin and wool left on the top steps. Winifred always wore slacks. The knee areas of the slacks were undisturbed. She landed more on her chest and head. It seemed more like she had really been given a shove and landed on the stairs midway down."

"First," George said quietly, "let's review the events, but keep the chronology straight. If they didn't die at the same time, don't connect the two events.

"And second, causing someone to fall down the steps doesn't always mean pushing. If you were standing at the top of the stairs and I wanted to make it look like you fell down the steps, I'd just stoop behind you and grab your ankles and pull them back towards me as I bopped your behind with my head, and you'd go down with your knee scraping one of the top steps and the heel of your hand trying to break your fall close to the top. So go back to that Friday Aunt Daphne fell. Was that the first unusual thing that happened? And how did Daphne get along with Roland?"

"Both aunts seemed... I don't know... to be afraid of him or not to trust him. He was their only living relative... he and his son Barry. So I guess they were conflicted. Also there was that business about the inheritance that his mother - who was their sister - had been cut out of the will. So there was an element of guilt or something. I can't define it. Something wasn't right. One time I heard Daphne say that she no longer had confidence that Roland would do what was right with the antiques. They were worried about Barrington... 'Barry' they called him. They said he had some kind of sickness which they never wanted to talk about, but right after I moved in I found those drug-withdrawal prescriptions. I figured that Roland didn't tell me because he didn't want to advertise that there's a drug addict in the family. But that seemed to jibe with keeping the wild kids away."

"I'm going to guess that the kid has a record and has already been suspected of stealing from the aunts. He's probably the reason you haven't been charged."

"How could I get sucked into Roland's confidence? I believed what I wanted to believe." She reached for a tissue and George quickly changed the subject.

"What about his wife? Did the aunts like her?"

"I got the feeling that they weren't too keen on Sybil. But they were well-bred ladies and didn't gossip."

"Did you get no clue that something was wrong?"

"I saw that while they had a nice mailbox, Roland picked up the mail at the post office. I thought that was odd until he explained that the post office was on his way home from work."

George looked at Akara. "Can you check that?"

Akara produced his iPad. "What was the name of his employer?" he asked as he connected to his incomprehensible "sixteen server computer cluster" that he kept at the temple.

"Advanced Alliance Associates."

Akara located the company and the address of Dalton Creek's one and only post office. He got the address of the Melbourne house and showed Carla that the post office was not on Roland's route home from work. In fact, Roland had to go considerably out of his way to get to it. "He did not want you to have access to the mail before he had an opportunity to cull it for any mail that might have something to do with his acquisition of the stolen goods. Were you questioned by the police?" Akara asked.

"Not about Daphne, but definitely about Winifred. For hours."

"Without a lawyer?"

"I didn't think I needed a lawyer. I hadn't done anything wrong!"

The tea was ready. George put the cups and saucers on the table with the pot of tea. Carla tried to pour, but her hand shook so badly that George took the tea pot from her. "You'll burn yourself," he said gently. "Let me do it. Go on with the story. Go back to after you went down to stay with them because of the home invasion."

"Anyway, as a gift to them that would make me feel more welcome, he bought them a chihuahua and I moved in with the dog. They adored her. She wasn't a baby but she had a bad leg so they babied her. Between the three of us we cared for that dog as though it were a human child. He bought her at a pet shop, and he also took her in for shots and bought all her food there. Winifred named the dog Bonbon." Carla began to cry. "This is all so insane! Why didn't I listen!"

"Don't beat yourself up about this. Frankly, it's better to be a trusting person and get fooled every once in a while than to live in the world as a paranoid person. Although, sometimes it's better to err on the side of caution." George, realizing that he had just given contradictory advice, quickly said, "Go back to where you moved in with the dog."

Carla began to sob so hard that George had to restrain himself from getting up and putting his arms around her. "Continue the story just as it happened," he said softly as he got up to put some ice cubes into a towel so that she could keep her eyes from swelling. "Here," he said, handing her the towel. "You don't want your pretty eyes to get all bloated."

Carla smiled weakly and murmured, "Thank you." She sighed deeply. She told him about the odd parking requirement, the need to use the bridal path, the sudden purchase of a car and his loan of $4000, the bizarre laundry service and the even more inexplicable catering arrangement.

"I began to wonder when I was going to return to his house, but it never happened. I just continued to live with the aunts.

"Then on Friday the 26th, Daphne had her fatal accident. Now, I was needed at the Buehler house, but still he would make no change in accommodations. Then it was learned that Daphne had changed her will and gave everything to her sister Winifred. Roland didn't ever figure that would happen."

"At that point he was his most dangerous. He was desperate."

"He told people he wanted Winifred to move in with him. And then the dog went missing on Thanksgiving."

"Do you see now that he wanted to give the public the unequivocal opinion that you lived with him - not them? He also knew you needed a car and rather than have you list your address improperly or give the house phone number for the dealer's credit department to call and check, he obviated the entire credit investigation. And, too, giving you the loan further indebted you to him. If you worked for someone else, it wasn't likely that he'd give you the loan. You'd have gotten it from his aunts. And no doubt, the dog was chipped to him at his house. To prevent the dog from favoring you and the aunts at any official test, he had to get rid of the dog. And you had no idea that he was setting you up?"

"Sure... after I heard him talk to the police and castigate me for sneaking down to their house and then trying to poison them with prejudicial statements about him and his wife and son, by blaming my thefts on them. Oh... he was so disappointed in himself for having been taken in by me!"

"Do you see that if you had openly lived with the aunts, you would not have known anything about him to tell them? You were able to poison them, he says, because you lived with him and were privy to his family secrets. If you had been their employee, you would have been canned before he had the opportunity to get the furniture. He also needed a diversion... the dog. He needed to keep their minds occupied and happy with you and the dog. Undoubtedly Daphne suspected him and changed her will. He might not have known about it. At any rate, he forged some kind of letter to a museum and decided to leave you home alone on Sunday mornings to sign for the removal and delivery. Go on."

"Daphne was buried, and the following week, while I was in school, the estate was inventoried - and that evidently included an appraisal of the antiques. Roland had brought Winifred up to his house so the different clerks and insurance people could work without any interference.

"Winifred didn't inherit everything. Daphne willed Roland a group of 'antiques' - pieces that apparently were reproductions of items that had already been stolen. She specifically gave him the 1740 decade of Poor Richard's Almanack, but they were only photocopies of the originals. It wasn't until after Daphne died that a neighbor told me about her suspicions during a condolence call that I heard about this switch. Until then I had not heard any mention of substituted fakes."

"Let me get this straight," George said. "She willed him fakes of the antiques he had already stolen? But she referred to them as antiques in the will? What a gal!"

"Yes. A bellows, silver boxes, copper pots... small things that a person could carry. Then on the next few Sunday mornings an old black walk-in van came and antique furniture pieces were exchanged for new pieces in the same style. I signed the delivery receipt. I remember the first piece was an 18th Century maple blanket chest."

"Did you get a copy of what you signed?" Akara asked.

"Yes, but I gave it to Roland."

"Did it have a logo on it? Some identifying heading on the sheet?"

"Yes. It said, 'Maryland Antiques Association' on it or something like that. I looked them up later and couldn't find any such business. There had been nothing written on the van."

Akara whistled. "And Aunt Winifred was at the small dog park. He is one slick character."

"Bonbon loved going to the park. Winifred would tell me about all her new chihuahua friends. Roland had asked me to stay home to watch the house and to be there for the museum truck."

George sighed. "Did you discuss the antique switch with Winifred?"

"No. Roland said not to since Daphne had written the letter and the sisters were not always in accord. I didn't want to start trouble since Winifred had responded so strangely to her sister's death. It was as if Daphne had died a martyr. 'Brave Daphne,' she called her."

"Were there other furniture switches... and were they all on Sunday mornings?"

"Yes. Eleven pieces total over three successive Sundays. Same old van and same two guys with a mover's dolly. I didn't think it was odd that the furniture was exchanged on a Sunday. For all I knew, that was how it was done here."

"Well, Carla, you have no proof that you merely were at the location of the transaction as an incidental receiver of the payment for the antiques and as the receiver of the new furniture copies. This sort of crime happens frequently, especially when the real owner of the antiques is old and has poor eyesight or maybe has Alzheimer's. The owner doesn't even know that the caregiver or relative has made the substitution."

"Yes... and I had no idea of what these antiques were worth. I looked on the internet and found that a chest from 1770 had sold for half a million dollars. I was dumbfounded. But at the time I just didn't put it all together. Hundreds of thousands of dollars worth of antiques... millions maybe... a desk that Winifred said George Washington used during the months that the Continental Congress convened in Maryland... furniture that had been around for several hundred years... priceless pieces of Americana... antique silver and copper pieces. The two of them talked about those things as though they were... well, not alive... but that they were with them, historically. The maid wasn't allowed to polish the furniture. Only they could. And they'd use old stuff in a bottle... some kind of oil. Once they were wiping the desk and said to me, 'Quill pens can be so drippy.' I didn't know what they were talking about."

"And you signed for all of it?" Akara asked.

"No, only the furniture. But I was getting suspicious. I began to notice that things that were supposed to be antique were not. There were brass candlesticks on the mantle that were made in India... and not in 1700s India.

"One day Winifred was telling me about the Revolutionary War and how Baltimore had acted as the Congressional seat when there was fear that Philadelphia would be attacked. She was giving me some history as she took a box of silver flatware from the sideboard. Service for twelve. 'The Founding Fathers actually ate with these pieces,' she said, opening the box. It was silver plate, not sterling and it was new stuff. I stood there and shook. I watched her get this god-awful look on her face as she rubbed her fingers over the bowls of a few spoons. She picked one up and held it so that she could see it with what was left of her eyesight. 'It's so shiny,' she said. 'Daphne must have had the maid polish them.' Then she quietly closed the box and put it back into the sideboard. Tears were running down her face. I felt terrible for Winifred. From what I had heard her say on the phone, I knew that it was Roland or Barry who had stolen the originals. Like an idiot, I still didn't think anyone could possibly blame me for the theft."

"Did you mention this to the police or to her attorney?"

"No. Winifred's mind was not impaired in any way. If she wanted to do that, she could have. It just wasn't my place. Instead I tried to make her feel better. I knew she loved Chopin's music and when the symphony advertised an evening of Chopin, I took her to the concert. She was thrilled. I took her again up here to the Academy of Music. The Philadelphia Orchestra was doing an evening of Beethoven and Wagner. Siegfried's funeral music... things of that sort. We stayed overnight in a place called Bryn Mawr with a friend she had gone to college with fifty years ago. We brought Bonbon with us. Winifred's friend watched her while we went to the Academy of Music. When we got back they sat up and talked late that night and then something changed in Winifred. She became secretive.

"Roland was angry with me for bringing her up here. I didn't think he'd object, seeing that she was so happy for a change, but he complained, loud and obnoxiously. Winifred heard us argue.

"While we were out looking for Bonbon, she had contacted her attorney, and he sent a car to pick her up. I waited in a coffee shop for her to return. Evidently it was then that she made a new will and named me sole beneficiary. She must have sat there until his secretary typed the will, so that she could sign it. She also dictated a letter asking me to give money to medical research for Retinitis pigmentosa and for young classical musicians... all at my own discretion. I didn't know about the new will and I don't know if Roland knew.

"The next day after I got back from the dog pound, looking there for Bonbon, Winifred was dead. Roland and Barry said they had come to the house an hour earlier to check on her and found her dead at the bottom of the cellar steps.

"I was asked to go to the police station to make a statement. Instead they questioned me over and over for six hours. Roland had said I lived with him and apparently only went down to the old ladies to visit them for some 'criminal' reason - to steal objects and to be on hand to oversee the illegal sale of antiques and the fake substitutes. He claimed that when Daphne left him pieces that turned out to be fakes, he took a closer look at the furniture and detected the well-made fakes. He had asked Winifred about it and she was so alarmed she insisted that she'd speak to me to see if I would give them back, and if I didn't, she'd call the police. That, apparently, was my motive for killing her."

"Carla, everything that he did was done to establish your guilt. I can guess that the medical examiner placed the time of death close to the time you left the house to go shopping, so that no matter when a store camera or the Animal Shelter camera picked you up, it was still possible for you to have pushed either one of them down the stairs just before you left the house."

"Yes. That's what they said. And when her attorney read the will - I now had at least 38 million motives."

"You need an attorney."

"I have no money to pay for an attorney. One of my classmates told me I should get a public defender."

George made an effort to sound purely reasonable. "Why don't you ask Dwight Ingram for the money? He would give it to you."

"I already feel too indebted to him. He only paid for my tuition because he felt indebted to me for having inspired him. I had gotten so enthusiastic about wanting to go back to school so that I could qualify for a surgical residency that it made him consider doing the same. If I could return to school after a fifteen year absence, he said he could, too. He enrolled in computer classes for architects and now intends to resume his practice. He says if it weren't for me, he would never have enrolled. He's so happy to be back in architecture again. Also, he knew some people associated with the medical school in Maryland so they let me be a late admission."

In an almost off-hand way, George said, "You could have called Beryl or me."

"You weren't returning my calls and I really didn't think I needed an attorney. I hadn't done anything wrong!" She began to sob so convulsively that Beryl came back to the kitchen.

After giving George a dirty look, Beryl said, "You may not need an attorney at all. But you should have one in case. We're licensed in Maryland, but we don't really know any Maryland attorneys to ask to give you a break. George can talk to some of his old friends down there to find out who's the best person to represent you." She narrowed her eyes and stared instructively at George.

Again, she tried to comfort Carla. "From here on in, you cannot do anything without an attorney's approval. When things have progressed this far, we'll need the agency extension of attorney-client privilege. Do you understand what I just said?"

"Yes. But how do I pay for an attorney?"

"First you find out how much he wants to represent you now, irrespective of criminal charges; and then what he thinks you'll need if you're tried. You come upstairs to my apartment with me while George makes a few calls. I'll make us tea and nuke some muffins."

Beryl, wanting to speak privately with Carla, asked Akara to stay downstairs for a few minutes.

Upstairs, Beryl asked, "Why don't you want to call Dwight?"

"I don't want to be indebted to him any more than I already am."

"That hasn't stopped you from seeking more help from George."

"I just can't ask Dwight Ingram for anything more. You should have been there at his house for Thanksgiving Dinner. It was a nightmare. Dwight and Chloe had come down the second weekend I was in Baltimore; and I got all tied up and was late meeting them. The trip was a waste for them. I called Chloe Ingram to apologize for my negligence and she responded by insisting that I come to Lake George for Thanksgiving. I expected a little dinner with her and me and Dwight and Danny. I didn't know that Dwight had begun a relationship with a girl from his computerized drafting class; and Chloe's boyfriend Danny had finally received his divorce decree. Since Dwight was bringing his new girlfriend, Chloe asked her brother to come, but he cancelled because he couldn't get flight connections. I was an uncomfortable 'fifth wheel,' at the festivities and was miserable and out of place throughout every moment of the two day visit."

"Frankly, you don't have an alternative - unless you want a public defender to represent you. And when thirty-eight million is at stake for Roland, you can bet he'll get great advice about where to find evidence against you."

"Do you really think I could end up in jail?"

"Jail? No. Prison? Yes. Carla! I think it's possible that you'll end up getting a life sentence. You need to get a more realistic view of your situation. You need Dwight's money. George is on the phone now trying to get you a lawyer. You say you want help. He's helping you. Now just do whatever he tells you to do."

Carla sat down. "I should have listened to George when he told me to let him check Roland out."

"Why didn't you ask someone for advice?"

"I did. I told Dwight about the job and he thought it was a great position."

"Dwight's an architect. He understands the interactions of steel and glass. George understands the dark side of interactions between human beings." Beryl took a deep breath. "Unless you know another man who's got the money to lend you, you're stuck with Dwight Ingram. This is no time for pride."

George, carrying his cellphone and a notepad, came through the open door of Beryl's upstairs apartment. "I talked to two retired cops down in Baltimore. Both gave me the same first choice for an attorney: Tom Alardi. Here's his number. The call has to come from you."

Carla Richards called the attorney's office and was told he'd call her back in half an hour. Beryl pushed her iPhone in front of Carla. "Keep your phone open. Here, call Dwight and ask him if he'd be prepared to front you for an attorney's fees if it should become necessary."

Carla called. "Hello Angel!" Dwight answered, seeing Beryl's caller ID. Beryl called, "Hello!" loud enough for him to hear as she grabbed George's arm and took him back down to the office. "Holler when you need us," she called as they left.

Tom Alardi returned Carla's call and listened to her recount the events of the past several months and said he'd call George immediately and discuss investigative expenses with him.

Alardi agreed to a $10,000 retainer to represent Carla for all pre-trial activity. If she were charged, there would be an additional cost for being her trial attorney; and if she were not charged and there was any refund of the retainer due, he'd give it. The costs of private investigation were a separate matter which would be left to Wagner & Tilson. Dwight Ingram said that he'd have $10,000 transferred immediately into Carla's bank account.

George came upstairs. "Now that everything is set to proceed, I'll ask Akara to come up here." He had not wanted Akara to sit in on any financial discussion for fear that he would automatically offer his own money. Serving a client without charge was one thing, but assuming a client's total legal costs was quite another. "I have a feeling we're gonna need a lot of computer hijinks to solve this case. Why don't you order some pizza."

"George," Carla said plaintively, "thank you for helping me."

George mumbled something inaudible as he went back down the stairs.

Akara Chatree looked at the pizza slices and sighed. "In Brazil," he said, "we eat our pizza with a knife and fork. Everybody laughs when Americans come into a pizza place and eat with their hands."

"I've got news for Brazil," Beryl said. "The germs add the most flavor."

"This is what I'm thinking," George said in his standard introduction to a plan of investigation, "Roland says Carla lived in his house and only visited the aunts. Let's prove that to be a lie. An additional person living in a house consumes more electricity and water. Let's get a year's worth of utility bills and show how the increase in the old lady's bills reflect the addition of another resident. Simultaneously, get a year's worth of bills from Roland's house and show that there was no concomitant increase in his utility bills."

George looked at Carla's phone. "With the houses only a kilometer apart your calls probably pinged off the same microwave tower. If there were two different towers, you could prove that you made your phone calls from one address or the other. It's a slim-to-none possibility that there were two towers. But let's check it out, anyway."

George continued. "Carla did not see the name of the furniture store that picked up the antiques and delivered the copies. She says the van was plain, black and old. So let's start by showing Carla a complete array of photographs of that walk-in type of van and see if she can more closely identify the make and model. We'll see where knowledge of an unusual vehicle takes us.

"We need to get descriptions of the eleven pieces that were stolen. No doubt there were bona fide appraisals made of the furniture both after Daphne Buehler's death and earlier - at some time in the past when they were insured. Alardi can get us a copy of the estate inventory back when Winifred and Daphne both inherited it, which would include all the antiques, and then the list of antiques which were there after Daphne's death. And finally the list that was made after Winifred's death. It would help if we could find one piece that was for sale someplace before Carla ever entered the picture. As to the furniture, we'll need the photographs of the real antique pieces as well as the fakes... since I would imagine that it's going to be easier to find who made the fakes than it is to locate the stolen pieces which are probably well hidden by now.

"Roland will likely wait a respectable amount of time before he files a claim for the lost furniture and maybe even some of the other smaller antiques. The insurance company will not rush to pay. We'll probably have to work closely with their investigators. Since Roland managed the aunts' business, I'm guessing that he is the beneficiary of the insurance on the original pieces.

"Roland may want to bolster his claim that Carla was paid for the antiques by showing that she suddenly had more money. Banks and ATM's have wall-to-wall cameras so he'd never risk hiring someone to impersonate her unless she had an identical twin. I'd look for him to secrete the money among her possessions... the old fashioned cookie jar or buried can. The cash would have to contain her fingerprints." He turned to Carla, "Did you ever handle currency of any kind for Roland?"

Carla Richards started to say that she had never handled money for Roland, but then she remembered that Sybil came home from a church Bingo game with a bag full of money and a story that the money had to be counted and recounted to be sure every penny was accurately reported. "I sorted and counted it right on the dining room table."

"They'd want to have you hide enough that you couldn't explain... say $8000 or $10,000. Was that amount there?"

"More. Sybil said that there was a big football game and a couple of the men who came to pick up their mothers after Bingo had just gotten paid off for their bets and tossed into the donation kitty a few thousand each."

"So what was the total you handled?" George asked, trying to be patient.

"Twenty-two thousand dollars and some change."

"Well, that tells us we're looking for a can that's bigger than a Prince Albert tobacco can. And when we find it, don't handle the container or the money with your bare hands... but do record every serial number of the bills. They may have sold an antique to get that currency. Without proper provenance papers, they would have sold it to a sleazy dealer. Money laundering being what it is, the cash may have originated in some illegal means. They wouldn't have had time yet to sell the bulk of the furniture. But they would have needed money to pay for the copies. Could they have taken a twelfth piece while Daphne was still alive?"

"Yes. Daphne missed a Windsor chair. How much could that have been worth?"

"An original? A small fortune!" Beryl exclaimed. "And quite enough to pay for the eleven copies."

George continued. "Unless they sold the pieces to an unscrupulous private collector, the stuff's not likely to hit the market for quite awhile. The lot is probably in a storage shed someplace. They'll have paid cash for the space so there's no point in trying to find a cancelled check or receipt. On the other hand, considering the value of the pieces, they'd have insured the storage locker's contents. And that insurance policy should have a paper trail... it was not likely to be in cash. We'll need to get into their records. And we'll also have to check every storage facility within a fifty-mile radius to get suggestions about the insurance companies who insure their locker contents.

"Now," George speculated, "that container of money is gonna turn up and very quickly I imagine. By the way, did he ever offer to cash your $300 paycheck? I'm guessing that he didn't."

"No. I always deposited it in my checking account."

"This establishes a consciousness of guilt. If you had come by the $22,000 honestly, you'd have put it into your bank account or paid off the $4K loan." George looked around the table. "Moving on," he said, "Roland may have resorted to theft and murder because he was having his own money problems. We'll need a complete rundown of his and Sybil's personal life. And I mean no stone left unturned for them to crawl under. And their kid, too. Barrington's 'sickness' may have cost them plenty. We'll need bank statements or other evidence that proves their money problems. What bad habits or mistakes did they make that cost them financially? For example, one of them may have dropped a hint of some kind. So, Carla, clear your mind and try to remember things said en passant. Maybe Sybil said something about a hat she once wore to the Kentucky Derby. That could mean they played the ponies. Or, he may have dissed a brokerage firm that huckstered a stock with a great future that then tanked, or, maybe he made a comment about the light sentence given to a man convicted of running a Ponzi scheme. Such comments may indicate his bad experiences.

George noted, "Only a few people ever visited the house. If the aunts suspected Barry, he might have unloaded the stolen items in his college town. His parents can't be happy with him horning in on their mark. There is probably trouble in Paradise. What can you tell us about the son?"

"Barry comes home for holidays. He goes to a small liberal arts college. I saw his books. It's something like Saint Alonzo College of Liberal Arts and it's near Hagerstown, Maryland."

"A cocaine problem usually isn't a person's only problem. Addictions to 'social' drugs sooner or later involve crimes of recklessness... gambling or burglary. And just because the kid may have a drug problem doesn't mean that Roland and Sybil Melbourne didn't lose money the old fashioned way... bad investments, Ponzi schemes, loans that weren't repaid, law suits that they lost. Sybil's jewelry, is it real or paste? Roland's car... is it leased or owned? Were they ever behind on their mortgage? Did any 'Past Due' notices come to the house? Try to remember things of that sort and write them down.

"Now, the aunts had friends, so we need to talk to them to find out what they said about Roland, Sybil, and Barry; and also how they alluded to Carla's living with them. Winifred was supposed to have changed after she stayed with her friend in Bryn Mawr. Let's find that friend."

Beryl pushed her little notepad in front of Carla. "Give us her name and address."

Carla shook her head. "I only knew her as Betty-Lou. Aunt Winifred called her Betty-Lou Bemberton or Pammerston... I never quite caught it. I don't know the street address because Winifred directed me. It was a big house and it sat by itself."

"You said the woman was blind," George interrupted. "How could she have directed you?"

"She told me to head for Bryn Mawr so I looked it up in a road atlas. I don't have one of those map things in my car. She told me to head for Lower Merion Township in Montgomery County and then when I got to the college she told me how many streets to go and when to turn right. She wasn't completely blind. She had some ten percent of her eyesight left."

Beryl held her hand up. "We can retrace the steps while it's still fresh in Carla's mind."

Akara tilted his head back and lowered a slice of pizza into his mouth. He bit off a hunk and, still chewing, said, "I'm thinking about that Windsor chair. Couldn't Roland have forged provenance papers? Couldn't he have represented himself as an agent of one of the aunts and then forged their signature on the paper? Why don't we zero-in on finding the Windsor chair. If Daphne missed it then he didn't have a copy substituted for it. My father has an account at Christie's. I can ask someone to see if a Windsor chair was on the market within the last year."

George noted. "Yes. With documentation, a reputable dealer may have handled the piece, but I doubt that Roland would go that route while the aunts were alive to refute the sale. We need to pull the Melbourne's telephone records to see if they spoke to a dealer or a storage company or the guys who had the black van.

"Where are their old records kept?" Akara asked.

Carla answered. "I think Roland keeps them all in his basement."

"Good," Akara mumbled as he continued eating.

George continued. "We'll need the names and addresses of any other friend they may have confided in. Did they have an address book?"

"Yes, but Roland took it," Carla said. "He said he needed it to send out death announcements... letters edged in black."

"What about their personal correspondence?" Beryl asked.

"The sideboard in the dining room is stuffed with letters and photographs. Maybe there are envelopes with return addresses."

"We're gonna need those names and addresses," George advised, "especially the recent letters in which they may have discussed Carla's presence as a live-in companion."

"The closest friends should probably have signed the Condolence Book at the funeral services," Beryl suggested.

"Where are the books?" Akara asked.

"I don't know," Carla replied. "I remember signing them at the funeral parlor, but I never saw either one after that. I don't think they were delivered to the aunts' house. And I'm not permitted back in to look. I've been living with a classmate. Roland said he had 'no choice' but to ask me to vacate his premises. He took my keys."

"Did they change the locks to either house?" Beryl asked. "And did you remember to file change of addresses with the post office and the Department of Motor Vehicles and your car insurance company?"

"Yes. My roommate advised me to do that immediately. I also notified the bank. Roland took my house keys right off my key ring. The caterer told me that the practice was that he would change the security codes, so I don't think he also changed the locks. I guess they still keep a key hidden in a fake stone, out in front of the house."

"We're going to need complete media research on Winifred and Daphne and on Roland, Sybil, and Barry. Any article written in which their names appear may link us to a friend or confidant or to one of the Melbourne's expensive habits or financial losses."

George continued his strategy. "I'm hoping that along with the post-Winifred inventory of the house there are separate photographs of the fakes. If there were no official photographs taken, we'll have to do an entry and get the shots."

Beryl handed Carla a pen and notebook. "Write down the name and address of the funeral parlor and the aunts' house and Roland's house, too. And his place of employment. Phone numbers. Anything you can think of. Sybil's employer... anything."

"I'll need to access Roland's computer," Akara said. "I can find out what he's up to if he uses it. I can also activate his audio and video. Chances are he keeps information in his work computer. Write down email addresses... for him and Sybil... and their office email addresses, too."

"No!" George said. "Do not touch Roland's computer. Ultimately we'll want to expose Roland as being the thief and killer. If we tamper with his private correspondence in any way whatsoever, we not only destroy our credibility we enhance his when he denies everything.

"The storage locker companies won't tell us who has a locker there but they will give the names of the insurance companies they use. With that information we may be able to track down the locker. The obstacle to such a search is that more than likely they used a fake company name with their license ID number or passport ID. There aren't that many pieces to require a big locker and they may not want to call attention to the contents by getting an appropriately large insurance policy."

Akara had a question. "I still don't get why it was so important for Roland to insist that Carla lived in his house?"

Beryl answered. "Because if she lived with the aunts, she'd have had time to develop a warm, caring relationship with them and it wouldn't be suspicious that they included her in their will - which is precisely what did happen. As a casual visitor, the picture changes."

Akara persisted. "What I mean is, why would Roland go through all this if he stood to inherit? They were old ladies. Why so much theft and killing so suddenly? Why couldn't he wait and retain the good-will of his aunts?"

"It's a question of urgency," Beryl said. "If you have a loose tooth that's infected, you know that it will eventually fall out. But if you've got a tooth ache, you don't want to wait. You proceed, and you usually proceed recklessly. Pull it out yourself. If Roland and Company had an urgent need, they were reckless. Count on it."

"Ultimately," George said, dismissing Akara's questions, "our best bet is to counter Roland's lie that Carla lived in his house and that the dog was his, and that he, his wife, his maid, and his son cared for it. He purchased its food - no doubt he has receipts to prove it. If the dog had an affection for Carla, that would be understandable. But the dog is not there to prove that it regarded Roland as an alien. We need to produce the dog."

"What can you tell us about the dog?" George asked Carla, signaling Beryl to write down the information.

"Roland bought Bonbon at the Dalton Pet Shop. Originally she came from Chalmer's Veterinary Service. The Vet kept her because she was born with a defective leg. She was pure bred. AKC registered. Finally he put her on consignment at the pet shop. I don't know if she was already chipped to the vet or to Roland... or how they work chipping data when a dog is re-sold."

"How old was the dog when Roland got her?"

"Eight months old."

Beryl agreed on the importance of finding the dog. "Roland may have needed to get rid of the dog, but he probably wouldn't have destroyed a valuable dog. He would have sold her to a puppy mill. Has she gone into heat yet?"

"It's possible," Carla said. "But I didn't think they'd breed a chihuahua until it was two years old."

"Reputable breeders wouldn't," George said. "But the puppy mills would. They'd C-section her, and since she's lame and can't be shown, they'd just keep her in a cage and breed her until she died."

"But her papers were still in the house after she 'ran away,'" Carla said.

"Irresponsible breeders don't care. If they didn't have her papers, they'd just put another AKC dog's papers on her... some dog that died. The papers don't evaporate at a dog's death. If they didn't do any doggie DNA, who would know?"

"Is she old enough now to have a first litter?" Akara asked.

"If she came into season," Carla replied. "It might kill her, but if she's fertile, I guess she could."

"Then we need a list of all the puppy mills in the area... or the not-so-reputable breeders of chihuahuas."

Akara offered, "I can get the list and we can get a chip scanner and secretly visit the breeding cages."

"Good idea," Beryl noted. "How long does the pregnancy last?"

"Two months," Carla estimated. "Then the puppies take another two months until they can be sold.... usually."

"That gives us the earliest window opening for puppies to be born at the end of January and the earliest puppy availability at the end of March," Beryl calculated, making notes in her book.

"So," said George, winding up the strategy session, "we find the furniture maker and we find the dog and the guys in the van and the storage locker, and we determine that Roland or Barry needed money badly, and we get the condolence books, and the insurance policy, appraisal, and final inventory, and some of Roland's basement records... finding an insurance policy on the stored pieces, and the utility bills.

Did I leave anything out?" The office phone rang. "I'll get it downstairs," he said.

As his footsteps trailed away, Beryl said, "We've got a lot of work to do. Most of it needs to be done in Baltimore and Hagerstown."

Akara Chatree interjected a suggestion. "Can you leave Carla with me? I'll talk to her here and also up at the temple and between the two of us, we'll remember a whole lot of stuff. I'll even follow her back to Baltimore."

"George has to meet with Tom Alardi in a couple of days," Beryl said. "Contracts must be signed."

"Then how about if I take Carla back and you drive her car down and come back with George? We're not busy in the temple. You guys tend to be intimidating. I think Carla will remember a whole lot more when she's more relaxed around me."

"That's ok with me," Beryl said, "but you have to take Carla first to get the street address of Winifred's friend out in Bryn Mawr. Call me with the number and a brief description of the house and if there's a name on the mailbox, get it. That's all you have to do there."

"Consider it done."

The precautions that George discussed, had, in fact, been followed by Sybil and Roland. They had the furniture delivered to a storage facility at the edge of town, renting the locker under the false name of "Dalton File Storage" and using, for identification, Sybil's passport number. They paid the rental in cash and had obtained an expensive combination lock to secure the locker door. Sybil and Roland did not immediately realize that Barry had returned home while they were discussing the locker. They had been speaking softly and doubted that he had overheard them discussing the storage facility and where they had written the combination. They had not mentioned that to deter anyone from determining that it was a lock's combination, they had used Spanish designations for "left" and "right" when they wrote the combination on the outside of a Miscellaneous file folder which they left in a basement file cabinet. No one, they were certain, would be able to figure out what the strange sequence of numbers and letters meant.

Akara followed Carla's directions and got to the Pemberton house in Bryn Mawr. He noted the street and house number and called Beryl.

Carla was sad and quiet the entire trip south. He didn't expect her to be talkative.

When he finally dropped Carla off at her roommate's quarters, he registered at the same motel that she had previously stayed in and called Sensei. He explained the situation to him and said, "I really need to understand why someone as intelligent as Carla Richards was so vulnerable to an obvious con-man like Roland Melbourne."

"Need," said Sensei. "In a word. She needed him and thought he was wonderful because he promised to fulfill that need."

"She needed George, too... and Dwight. Yet she evidently wasn't such a big fan of either one of them."

"Last week's need is like last week's fish. I'm not saying that Carla thought to herself, 'Yeah, but what have you done for me lately?' As George and I both know, she's a classy lady. She's not self-centered... not at all.

"But each new crisis in a person's life brings new needs. And at the moment, her needs were for a place to live and a salary by which she could be independent of those other people whose charity fulfilled her previous needs. She was simply being human. He was a crook and a crook is usually a master of the fine art of seeming to be wonderful at the *dawn* of any relationship. Twilight usually leaves the other fellow feeling lucky to be alive. But he was a master of that vital first impression.

"George Wagner knew what Carla is only now beginning to understand: external appearances are a lousy way to judge a person's character.

"When taste and style and other elements of refinement, which are assumed to be an individual's personal expression of quality, can easily be copied by an opportunist, then presenting such taste and style becomes simple mimicry; and when techniques of inducing favorable responses in human interactions - the smile, the eye-contact, the handshake and deferential attitude - can be deliberately acquired in order to exploit the advantages of a good first impression, we usually find ourselves being tricked by what is false and then denigrating the less engaging presentations of those who may possess far more knowledge, skill, and virtue.

"These First Impression masters make their eyes crinkle at the corners - a sure sign of genuine joy - when they smile at someone. Their handshakes have the precise firmness and duration that science has determined will produce maximum confidence and affinity. They have a natural deference to rank... never obsequious... just respectful.

"They dress well - never fastidiously which might be considered intimidating - but always with a conservative appropriateness. The correct garment never fails to put a person at ease.

"You can't pick up a magazine but that there's an article in it about how to make a good first impression. In other words, any guy can learn how to trick people into believing that he's a man of integrity and self-respect. If a man has to learn it, he doesn't have it to begin with. A normal man knows how to shake hands when he meets someone. He automatically smiles when he's happy. He doesn't need to fake it.

"It's like finding a hundred dollar bill in the gutter. If it's a genuine bill, fine. If it's not, then the excitement lasts only until it's discovered that the bill is counterfeit. But by then it may be too late. The person may go into an innocent person's shop and buy something for twenty-five dollars and give the clerk the fake one-hundred dollar bill and receive seventy-five genuine dollars in change.

"With the fake person, secrets might have been shared or money lent; and then the faker's abuses have to be tolerated for fear that he will blab the secret or fail to repay the loan. Worse, the person may have vouched for his so-called good friend, helping him to get a job in which he's incompetent or crooked. He or his friends can co-sign the crook's note and wind up having to pay it when he skips out. This was Carla's problem. She immediately believed in Roland's integrity. He had none. He stuck her with the tab. The rule is 'Don't have friends. Just be friendly.'"

Akara sighed. "Nobody needs to tell me about the perfidy of friends. I got taken in too. I tried to help someone and was nearly killed for my trouble. Well, she's got my sympathy. Somebody helped me, and I'm gonna help her."

TUESDAY, DECEMBER 18, 2012

Beryl pulled into Tarleton House's driveway to have breakfast with Lilyanne Smith early... before George could be aware that she was gone. Even at 7 a.m. the rush hour traffic was accumulating and she barely escaped the worst of it.

Lilyanne's health, while still much improved over the state she was in nearly a year before, was not sufficiently good to allow for breast feeding and the Smiths therefore employed two nannies to care for the baby. Since she lost no sleep through the night, she was able to look surprisingly good - freshly showered and coiffed at such an early hour. "Imagine," Lilyanne said proudly, "a month old and already he sleeps four hours at a stretch, the night nanny said."

"That's quite an accomplishment," Beryl said in complete sincerity. "I don't think my Jack slept four hours straight at night until he was at least three months old."

After breakfast they discussed paternal grandparents.

"My father asked the consul in Vienna to approach the Haffners with the photos of me and the baby. I got the professional proofs back on Monday and frankly there were only two I'd consider so I didn't have to bother you for an opinion. Anyway, that day they were electronically sent to our most excellent consul who printed them out in matte finish, and on Tuesday he met with the very formal - let us say, 'rigid' - grandparents. Fortunately he had used the embassy limo to drive up to their house or else they might have thrown him out - at least that was his opinion.

"Then the fireworks started with their attitude. Surely he didn't expect them to accept the photographs as 'evidence.' He objected to the use of the word. He said, 'We are not here to discuss legal matters. And

I am not here in an official capacity. The child's maternal grandparents are personal friends. If you want the photographs, you may have them. If you don't, I'll take them back lest they fall into the wrong hands.'"

"He is good," Beryl said approvingly.

"Naturally they wanted to keep them but asked him to understand that they'd like DNA confirmation. They asked how their representative could reach me to take a sample from me and the baby. He told them, and given the time difference, it was still morning when they called New York and asked someone who was attached to Austria's UN delegation to fly down here and get samples of the baby and me. I guess they wanted to check out our little domicile before they committed themselves to American Trash. And probably when their DNA collector reported that we were not destitute and living under a bridge, Herr Haffner called and spoke to my father who couldn't understand the man's English. So he put my mother on the phone. I was at the obstetrician's office having my first postpartum visit.

"My mother succeeded in getting Eric's mother to come to the phone and fortunately the two of them could speak French to each other. I had told my mother that if she discussed my son's father with anyone at all, I'd leave home with the baby. My parents were never to mention the Cayman Islands. But to tell the truth, they knew nothing about who or what I had met in the Caymans. Frankly, I think they thought the baby was George's. My dad tried to speak with George half a dozen times, but he couldn't get him to respond.

"Meanwhile, they had a hairbrush of Eric's and the accountant who sent him the remittance money every month had years worth of envelopes in which Eric would send his yearly income tax forms or whatever they call them. So get this! They said they could not be sure that the saliva on the envelopes was actually Eric's. And if they could not get a DNA result from hair follicles on the brush, they would not accept the saliva test as valid. So the man who got our samples had to explain to them that yes, they could, if they themselves submitted to DNA tests. He added, 'Assuming of course that you are both biological parents of Eric.' They nipped that potential slur right in the bud - if I may mix a metaphor. And six DNA tests were done *tout de suite*. Mine; Baby Eric's; Eric's hairbrush; Eric's envelopes; and each of Eric's parents.

"My mother was hysterical laughing at them. Yesterday was D-Day or DNA Day, and when all the tests added up to a Haffner grandchild, they wanted to come here with an attorney. This attorney calls; and my dad says, 'I will meet with you in my office when my attorney is present, but I will not countenance the Haffners' presence in my home if they require legal advice to be my guest. You have overstepped the bounds of propriety. My good wife and I are offended.' And he hung up. I was so proud of him.

"Naturally Erica - yes, Eric was named for his mother - called back immediately and spoke soothing words to *ma mere*. The upshot of all these intrusions into my life is that my mom invited them here for Christmas dinner. So Mrs. Haffner says, 'I'll speak to my husband about it and let you know.' This, of course, did not sit well with my mom, so she said, 'Well, I have a staff to inform and if there is to be time for discussion there will not be time for preparation. Perhaps we can arrange an *Easter* dinner.' Whereupon Mrs. Haffner accepts for her husband. The gang will all be here on Christmas Day and I'm begging you to come to preserve my sanity. I know it's short notice, but I implore you... save my neck. Please come for Christmas dinner. Please, Beryl."

"No! It would break George's heart. Don't ask again. George is my mentor, my partner, my best friend. If I could bring him, I'd be here in a heartbeat. Without him, I wouldn't dare come to within thirty miles of this house."

"Life is so complicated. The Haffners will be here next Sunday the 23rd. We will decorate the tree together. They're bringing decorations that Eric will remember - 'if he sees the photographs' his mother said. I keep remembering Eric saying that he'd let his mother hold our beautiful baby for a minute and then he'd take him away from her and leave her crying. He'd say, 'You thought you destroyed me... well, you didn't. And here I am happy with a beautiful family and you are as miserable as you have ever been.'

"And you picked an early time to come today probably because you don't want George to know you're here."

"Yes. That doctor he had a little fling with has been in town. She's potentially got legal problems and we're on the case. He thinks I'm interviewing a neighbor of yours over in Bryn Mawr. Which, in fact, I must leave now to do."

"What is her name? And is she in town now?"

"Carla Richards. She's a physician. She's taking medical courses down in Baltimore to get ready for a surgical residency. Akara Chatree, that young Brazilian-Thai priest who's living at the temple, is taking her back to Baltimore." Beryl got up to leave.

"Tell me this before you go. Do you think I should show Eric the baby?"

"Lily, if you return to the Caymans you may be held as a material witness to several serious crimes. According to George, the *Sesame*, a million dollar yacht, was left in Cayman Brac when the two of you left the island. Two of the owners were missing and one of them was dead with a harpoon nailing him to a wooden wall. Eric may be dead or in jail or under suspicion. Anybody who was there at the time of the incident is likely to be questioned and possibly held. That means you and George. Neither one of you can return to the island."

"I've been in touch with Captain Quintero. He had asked me to leave word with the harbor master in Grand Cayman. I told him I was safe at home and sent him a letter care of the Barcadere Marina office. We've written. I could meet Eric at sea."

"What? You and the baby on his boat and Eric rows a dinghy over to you? No, Lily. You're involving innocent people in what may turn out to be a murder case. Eric has a passport. You can't prevent him from coming here, and as long as the accountant keeps sending him money every month, now that the paternal cat is out of the bag, Eric will know about the baby. You have got to think things through to all possible consequences."

"I know I know. Acting impulsively is what nearly got me killed in Cayman Brac. I need to talk to Sensei. Will he see me?"

"Yes. He doesn't report to George. It was your father who told George you were consulting with Sensei."

"I didn't know that."

"Talk to Sensei. You'll be doing him a favor... taking his mind off his worries about 'his lady' la *belle* Sonya Lee. He hasn't heard from her in months and he's frantic. And for the next few days, at least, George and I will be in Baltimore. So if you want to ride out to the temple and not have to worry about George showing up, you can. He and I will both be down there this afternoon."

Akara Chatree, wearing a suit and tie, slowly drove past the Boynton Funeral Home and noticed something that would be helpful. "I see that the funeral folks like privacy," he informed Carla. "They've let shrubs and trees cover the windows. They don't stop to think that the same shrubs that prevent people from looking in windows, prevent people from seeing what is between the shrubs and the windows, namely, a burglar."

A sign on the lawn indicated that services were about to commence for the late Jennsen Foster, Esq. A few dozen people were approaching the limestone staircase to pay their last respects to the gentleman lawyer.

Akara parked his new red Corvette and told Carla that since there was too much danger of her being recognized by someone, she should wait for him in the car while he "checked out the place." He instructed her to be patient.

He scribbled his name in the condolence book and sat in the rear of the chapel viewing room, and when he supposed that there could not possibly be more clichés spoken about the old man in the coffin and that by sheer attrition the eulogies would soon end, he went to the men's room to scope out the layout.

He passed a secretarial office that was filled with ordinary office equipment and filing cabinets. He continued on to the owner's office and was startled to see an entire wall filled with shelves that contained all the condolence books that had been used since the establishment had opened for business a century before. He stepped into the office far enough to see a picturesque bay window at the room's far end, and the owner's desk, framed in light, that was strategically placed so that, according to a brochure he picked up and read, behind him "wisteria clusters hang down to whisper messages of hope to morning glories whose ear-trumpet blossoms plead to hear words of consolation." A desk and straight-backed chair had been supplied for "a bereaved family member" to use if he or she wanted to consult the books for any reason. He noted the design and size of the most current books. Someone tapped on his shoulder. "May I help you?" a woman - probably the secretary - asked.

Akara was startled. "My grandparents are looking for a suitable place to hold a funeral service, and I'm afraid I was just snooping a bit." He smiled broadly. "Where is everybody?"

"It's just offices on this side. Everyone's out to lunch at the moment - except the staff that does the actual preparation. They work through the night downstairs. The casket display room is on the other side of the chapel. We hold services from 8 a.m. to 10 p.m. And there's always someone here to answer the phone."

"That's good to know," Akara said. "Where can I find the men's room?"

He followed the direction to which her hand pointed and decided, as he entered the men's room, that the tall rhododendron bush outside the bathroom window was indeed fortuitous.

He began to think scientifically. He had noted that the entrance stairway was approximately two meters in height. He calculated that the mens' room windowsill was a meter above the floor. He'd need a 12 foot ladder at least to safely reach the sill. The ladder would be aluminum and his best bet, if he intended to return for the books at night, would be to buy a can of flat black spray paint to make it less noticeable. He would go to a stationery store and find identical condolence books or ones that were similar.

The window's lock was an old-fashioned flared sash lock. He would unlock the window and then return at night to exchange the books. After they had been studied and photocopied, he'd re-enter the premises and swap the books back. He flushed the urinal and flipped the window lock to its open position, and left the room not realizing that he had activated a silent alarm. He returned to the chapel, and hearing the same clichés being recycled, he left the pew and headed for the door only to come face to face with uniformed security guards.

Akara was forced back into the chapel along with a few other mourners who were trying to make a graceful exit. "We've gotten a report of an intruder," the head guard announced to the startled attendees.

"Is this some kind of joke?" the widow Foster protested. The man at the podium had a confused look that was mistaken for guilt as everyone looked to him for an explanation. Soon the congregation was on its feet and the mortician was telling everyone to stay calm because there had to have been a mistake.

A former colleague of the deceased began to act as though he were giving an opening statement to a jury. "What, I ask you," he gestured to the guards, "could possibly be stolen in a mortuary?"

Someone who had made a recent inquiry about caskets shouted, "Christ! They've got a hundred thousand dollars worth of caskets in that showroom!"

A few people snickered. The laugh relieved the tension. "Who'd want to steal a casket?" somebody asked.

A wag quipped, "Look for six guys walking slow."

The owner begged for order and for everyone to remember the solemnity of the occasion as the widow repeated that whatever it was that was happening was an outrage. Fortunately, a guard found the open window latch in the men's room and also a few innocent boys who were in the lobby who were quickly blamed. Without saying a final goodbye to the old attorney, the congregation dispersed.

It was at 10 a.m. of that sunny and brisk Tuesday morning that Beryl, driving Carla's car, pulled into the driveway of the old mansion in Bryn Mawr. The houseboy answered the door, and as Beryl handed him her business card, she said, "I have an appointment with Ms. Elizabeth Louise Pemberton."

"Please come in," the houseboy said, stepping aside and gesturing that she should enter. "Madam is expecting you." She followed him into the morning room.

"Come in, my dear," the smiling old lady said, "and please share a cup of tea with me. It's just now finished steeping. And there are wonderful cookies here." She poured Beryl a cup of tea.

"Now, what did you want to know about our dear Winifred? I was so sorry to have missed her funeral service. No one informed me."

The tea was jasmine and required no milk or sugar. Beryl sniffed its aroma and nodded appreciatively. She sipped the brew and then returned the cup to its saucer. "Miss Winifred learned something here that made her want to disinherit Roland. Can you possibly tell me what that was? Roland has claimed that Dr. Carla Richards did not live with Winifred and that the dog Bonbon was his dog - not Winifred's or Daphne's dog. These are absolute lies."

"Do you think Roland pushed Winifred and Daphne down the stairs?"

The question, unequivocally direct and substantive, startled Beryl. She blinked. "Either he, his wife, or his son may have done it. I don't believe that under the circumstances of the theft of so many of their antiques - thefts which apparently took place over a period of months or years - anyone should automatically assume the two ladies just happened to fall at what seems to be a critical time in Roland's life."

"Yes, Roland and Barry were stealing from them. Barry has one of those drug diseases. He goes to be cured and says that he's cured, but then he goes right back into the opium den or wherever he goes to get cocaine. And he has to steal to pay for his habit. Roland and his wife cover up his crimes with their own."

"Do you know how the sisters first found out that they were stealing?"

"Do you know what a Cape Cod lighter is?"

"I'm afraid I don't."

"It's a metal container that holds maybe a pint of oil, and immersed in the oil is a porous stone that is secured at the end of a long wire handle. The stone soaks up the oil and then when someone wants to light a fire, they insert the stone at the bottom of the wood. Naturally the oil burns easily and the fire starts.

"Winnie had a one-of-a-kind Cape Cod lighter that was made by an obscure apprentice craftsman in Massachusetts. His name was Piers Grover and he died at age 17 in 1760. Over his name Piers had inscribed, 'Keep me full and I will warm thee' on the poorly wrought container. Winnie brought it to school - we laughed about the saying and kept a spare set of room keys in it. It became a kind of motto to us. This was right after the War. Fifty years later one of us girls, Diane Henderson, saw that same Cape Cod lighter for sale in an antique store for $25. She bought it and called Winifred and Daphne who were dumbfounded. At first they thought it must be a duplicate until they looked for theirs and couldn't find it although they had seen it a month before when they polished the brass. Naturally they bought it back from Diane. That was nearly two years ago.

"Winifred says that Barrington would visit them, usually claiming to be bringing them cookies that he said his mother made but which were store-bought, and would act suspiciously. The Cape Cod lighter put them on their guard.

"Then last year in the summer, Barry was at the house and Daphne immediately noticed that a pair of antique candlesticks were gone. She was angry and confronted him, threatening to report the theft to the police. He returned the candlesticks, and then, two days later, he was beaten up so badly he had to be hospitalized. Sybil was vicious. She blamed Winifred and Daphne for having so much wealth and yet denying the boy the means to save his life. He had been threatened by thugs who demanded he pay them money. He was scared, she said, and that's why he stole the candlesticks. He wasn't even recognizable, Daphne said. The sisters felt terrible. They assumed that he owed debts for foolishness... cards or dice. They didn't know about his drug use.

"He started school in Hagerstown, and the aunts paid his tuition and his rent in an apartment; and on Thanksgiving Day dinner he asked to be excused from the table to go to the bathroom and it was nearly half an hour when he returned and when they got home Staffordshire plates were missing along with a silver box. Daphne had said his nose was red and that he claimed to have a cold. They didn't want him to get beaten up again. They were still debating whether to tell Roland when Christmas came and once again he left the table and didn't get back for half an hour and when they got home two Revere pots were missing. Before they could tell Roland, he told them that Barry was in the hospital. He had overdosed on those drugs.

"Roland said he had not recovered from the beating. So the girls paid to have him admitted to a rehab center for six months. Then Daphne saw Roland examining some of their old books - they had ten years worth of Poor Richard's Almanacks, the entire 1740 decade - and when Daphne later looked for the books, they were gone. Photocopied versions were in their place. Roland had made a few bad investments. They must have been big and bad to need those Almanacks to cover the loss. The Almanacks were particularly hurtful. Winifred couldn't watch television, and Daphne would read the Almanacks to her - she had done so for years! I think every line Franklin wrote was committed to memory. The photocopies were like copies of paintings. They looked alike, but Benjamin Franklin's hands never touched them.

"They talked to Roland who begged for forgiveness and promised to try to get the Almanacks back. He said that he figured that as their sister's son he was due to inherit the things anyway. But the girls said they had intended to give him stocks and bonds and real estate. The antiques they wanted to give to the Smithsonian or one of those museums. They were angry. That's when Daphne changed her will.

"And then at this year's August birthday dinner, Barry was out of that rehabilitation hospital, and just before dinner Roland went to the store, and when the girls came home a pewter tea set was missing. Then Sybil's expression when she was looking at a piece of what was supposed to be Revere's work let Winifred know that more substitutions had been made. And finally when Winifred showed Carla the sterling flatware it seemed to be too shiny and she said that Daphne must have just polished the set, but she knew that it had been switched. She then immediately decided to change her will, disinheriting Roland.

"I had told both of them to make a concerted effort to give the museums the pieces as soon as possible. I think they were getting ready to do it finally. But then Daphne fell to her death and Winifred feared that Daphne's death was no accident. She didn't know that Daphne had told me about the missing Almanacks. Then Winnie told me the strangest thing. She had confronted Roland about the sterling flatware set and he broke down and cried. He admitted that he had taken it from her but then Barry had stolen it from him and paid off a $28,000 dollar debt with it. It was worth, literally, hundreds of thousands of dollars. Maryland had been the seat of the Continental Congress for several months and that service was used at the dinner table by the Founding Fathers of this republic.

"And that's what we discussed on the night of the Symphony and later on the phone. I begged her to change her will and to give those pieces to the museums as soon as possible. She changed her will, but she never lived to donate anything to the museums. Maybe she didn't know which pieces were genuine and which weren't.

"She trusted Carla and thought that by giving her the estate she'd sort everything out and do right by them. She knew that Roland wouldn't.

"And now you tell me that Carla is going to be blamed. I will happily testify for her. Please tell her that."

"Ms. Pemberton, I beg you not to discuss this with anyone. If you have someone you can go away to visit for a few weeks... some distant place... tell no one where you are going... please go. Your life is in danger. Two people have been killed and a fortune in heirlooms have been stolen. You have my card. Don't hesitate to call me and don't fail to stay on guard."

"Oh, dear," replied Betty-Lou Pemberton, "I'm afraid I've already discussed the situation with quite a few of our old friends. I hope they'll be discreet."

As Beryl left she first called Tom Alardi and told him of the conversation with Ms. Pemberton and also of the elderly lady's willingness to testify to her meeting with Winifred. Then she called George who immediately began the drive south to Baltimore. He agreed to wait for her outside the motel. Akara had already checked into a double room at the motel. The plan was that George and Beryl would check-in together, possibly into the room next to Akara's and then George would simply use Akara's room.

As they were checking in, a few visitors and the desk clerk were laughing as they discussed a raid on the Boynton Funeral Parlor. "Maybe they were serving a writ of Habeas Corpus," one quipped. "You have the body!"

George asked, "Did you say, 'Boynton'?"

"Yes, they can keep the body, but the widow wants her money back."

The disturbance made the evening news as reported by a TV trainee and cameraman who had followed the security guards as they responded to the mortuary's false alarm.

Beryl and George sat in their motel room and watched television. They got a good look at the back of Akara Chatree as he entered his new red Corvette.

"Get that boy on the phone," George said through clenched teeth, and Beryl called the young priest's number.

WEDNESDAY, DECEMBER 19, 2012

"George," Tom Alardi began, "I'm gonna ask you outright. Here in town yesterday, we had a scene of pandemonium at what should have been a dignified funeral service for a much loved attorney. Now, the funeral parlor was the same one that was used for both Daphne and Winifred Buehler. Somehow a window latch had been deliberately opened and security guards stormed the ceremony. As it happens they took the license numbers of every vehicle that was parked in the area. They do that, you know, as a matter of course. And there was a shiny new Corvette there with Pennsylvania plates and a nice-looking dark-haired young man who left the services and drove away in it. I took the trouble to run those plates and found out that the fellow who owns that car lives a few houses down from your office. Is he your employee?"

"Tom," George Wagner replied, "let me assure you that he is not yet my employee. He is not licensed by the state and he did not do what you suspect him of doing at my suggestion. I am hoping to train him because, Tom, this is a new age we're living in and that young man has a PhD in computer science - which probably accounts for the obvious fact that he has no common sense. I'm tryin' my best. It is easier to teach an intelligent man like him how not to act like an idiot than it is for intelligent men like us to learn computer science."

"George, I was going to say that under no circumstances would I link my name to your investigative agency. Trying to break into a funeral parlor would not have been an auspicious way to begin a professional relationship. However, it just so happens I have a highly technical problem involving computers that I would like to keep private. I am wondering if we can reach some kind of financial accord. Can I barter for your trainee who seems more attractive to me now that I know he doesn't seem to know much about ethics?"

"Tom, he is outside in your waiting room. I'm sure we can come to some kind of agreement involving his expertise regarding your problem, and your expertise regarding Carla Richards' problem. The extent of the services we can leave until later. You're a man of integrity and I'm sure you'll be fair."

"George," Alardi said, standing up to shake hands, "let's see if we have a deal. Call your trainee in here and then leave us to chat privately. I may have to represent him in the matter of the false alarm at the Boynton Funeral Home - the widow may sue - so be sure he has a dollar on him. These kids love plastic too much."

George nodded, walked to the door, opened it and said, "Dr. Chatree, your attorney is ready for you now." He reached into his pocket and extracted a dollar bill. "Here," he said, handing it to Akara as the young scientist entered Alardi's office.

Attorney-client privilege having been established, Alardi stated his problem. "Somebody in my office is using my email address on the Mac computer in our private reference room to send out nasty emails that contain confidential information and a lot of salacious lies. For high-profile cases or the occasional case that involves national security, we keep reference material and files in this separate research room. The computer in there will accept and record as the sender any one of the six email addresses that belong to me and my five associates. After the person sends nasty stuff he deletes it and empties the trash. Somebody told me that a forensic computer examiner could retrieve the communications. Is that possible?"

"Usually you can retrieve the data. Not always, though. If national security is involved, you can let the feds mess with it, but then you'll let them see everything else that's in it."

"Thus far it's been mostly the personal attack stuff of character assassination and tidbits about clients or where an investigation is heading. A recent one tipped off an adversarial attorney about our defense strategy at trial."

"The same reservation applies. If you already know what the emails reveal, why risk subjecting the entire computer to someone's analysis?"

"Good question. I keep changing the password to my mail account. I've advised my associates to do the same; but somehow, someone's getting the new passwords. How is that possible?"

"The easiest way for a layman to do it is to observe the person's hands as he types in the number. A camera can be hidden inside a book, a vase of flowers, an overhead sprinkler, a lamp, a smoke detector, a flower pot, a picture frame, in anything that can hide a tiny camera. By slowing down the speed of what it records, he can watch and see the key that is being touched and just get the password that way."

"Hmm. I also tried letting the video camera run, and all they did was come up behind it and put a metal thing over the lens area. I thought about installing a secret camera in the room, but I still couldn't tell if what I was watching was real communication or the troublemaking kind. I ought to throw the goddamned machine out the window!"

"It isn't your computer that is sabotaging you. The person can hamper your ability to use your computer and then just use the U.S. mail to send out the spurious communications. You need to identify the person. You could install a device that sends the duplicate communications - plus a command not to obey the delete key or activate the function that empties the trash - but then you'd have placed the information outside of your secure reference room; and that still won't tell you who typed it."

"What would you do?"

"There are so many variables that I don't know about. Your Mac can be operated from your iPhone and iPad. Maybe others can do it, too. If you want to operate in stealth and maybe discover your attacker and then counter-attack, you could install a listening device that would let you hear and record the computer talking to itself. Each number and letter has a unique sound. The rhythm of the key sequence is also unique to everyone. A good typist, of course, types at a precise rhythm. But the people you're speaking of are not professional typists. There are many other ways to get information. These are just examples."

"What do you mean? Listen to it talk? Do you mean sounds like the beeps of a digital phone number? Each number has its own sound?"

"Well... yes. Each key produces a different electronic sound, and if you know the frequency of each sound you can interpret the message. Let's say that someone is typing a letter and your listening device captures the individual sound frequencies in sequence. Then you do what cryptographers do. If you know the person is typing English text, you correlate a specific sound with the general usage of that sound in English. For example, the most used letter in English is 'E' - so the frequency that is most often recorded will likely be an 'E' - and the second most used letter is 'T' so the second most used frequency will likely be 'T' and the third most used is 'A' and so on.

"Once you establish the frequency it's like doing a puzzle. When you reconstruct the document, do a word analysis. Record all oddities... words, grammatical errors or preferences, punctuation, spelling, phrasing and overall style. I once knew a woman who was suspected of writing a certain article and she looked at the opening paragraph and got indignant. 'I never begin a sentence with an appositional phrase!' You know what I mean... 'A well-groomed gentleman, Jack wore spats.' The Unabomber was caught because he repeated phrases. You would have samples of legitimate communications that you could compare the troublemaking ones to. And the rhythm of the strokes would be unique to each person typing."

"I'd get various communications and sort them for rhythm and look for these 'peculiarities' in the writings of my associates and staff."

"Yes."

"Is there no faster way?"

"If the reference room is locked, how many people have a key to it?"

"Five of my associates and my secretary."

"Lock the reference room and call a meeting of all of them who are on the premises. Leave the computer on and spray the keyboard with a kind of fluorescent-type spray that is visible only with special eyeglasses. Discuss a case and then make up something sort of scandalous about your private life, and then suddenly remember that you need another document, and ask the guy you most suspect to go into the reference room's paper files and extract a document - one that may take a few minutes to locate. Put the glasses on when he comes back. You'll see if he touched the keyboard."

Tom Alardi squinted, pursed his lips, and nodded. "We're having an associates meeting today at 4 p.m. Can you get me a can of that stuff and the glasses before then?"

"Sure. Can you get me the insurance files on the Buehler house antiques?"

"I'll race you. So, Dr. Chatree, since you want to swap my expertise for yours, go out there and tell Carla Richards to come in here. I'd like to speak to my client. Oh... as your attorney, may I suggest you stay away from funeral parlors and keep your nose clean."

"Gotcha.'"

"Where were you?" Beryl asked as Akara returned to the motel at 2 p.m.

"I was doing a private favor for Mr. Alardi." He handed her a manila envelope. "Here are the insurance files you and George wanted."

George looked through the contents of the envelope. "Here's the original 1975 inventory. With individual photographs of the antiques! And here's the inventories taken after both Daphne's and Winifred's deaths. The furniture is all there in Daphne's list - with the exception of a Windsor chair - but there are—" he began to count, "more than two dozen small items that are missing from the antiques' list. There are no photographs of the fake furniture." He looked up. "Why would there be? Jesus. Roland also has an insurance policy based on the 1975 list. The policy was re-written in 1990 when an insurance company appraiser went to the aunts' house and verified the existence of the entire collection and underwrote it at $7 million. Roland's the beneficiary."

"And after Winifred's death?" Beryl asked.

George sifted through the pages. "After Winifred's death it was a simple matter to inventory the contents of the house. There were only a handful of antiques that dated to Colonial times. Some Civil War stuff, that's all."

"So what," Akara asked, "is Roland's game?"

George, calm finally after the funeral parlor debacle, resumed the role of mentor. "Do a Zen meditation and put yourself in the position of each of the principals. This is kind of a Jungian 'active imagination' exercise. Clear everybody else's motives and excuses and prejudices out of the picture. Whenever a 'possession' is involved... whether it's of a person, place, or thing, the first thing you have to consider is your principal's sense of 'right' to possess it. He or she feels 'entitled' to it. In conjunction with that is a feeling of 'justice.'

"So don't have the mind-set of looking for a criminal. The kinds of mistakes criminals make are not the same kind of mistakes people make when they honestly believe that they're entitled to the property in question.

"You'll have to become aware of certain universal truths which have nothing to do with Zen or any other religion. In this case the first truth is that the person who believes that he is entitled to something will do everything possible to protect his entitlement. In the case of an inheritance, from the moment he first learns or believes that it will be his someday, he takes a proprietary attitude towards it. He tries to limit people's access to it since he fears they may disturb or diminish the bequest. He also seeks to limit contact with the present owners since outsiders may influence them to change the bequest. That is a universal truth. Applying it to Roland, you can see that in his mind, everything those old ladies had in their house was his. He was the only son of three daughters who were slated to inherit their parents' money and collection.

"Now consider the personal injustice he felt. As a teenager he knew wealth and social position. He went to the best schools and did well.

But before he entered college, his grandmother died and disinherited his mother. She didn't approve of his father. But why, he asks himself, does she punish his mother and him for the actions of his father? She may not have wanted his father to get his hands on her money, but there were other ways she could have prevented that. Instead, she punished his mother and, indirectly, him. This he sees as a kind of crime committed against him, and he sees his aunts as part of the criminal conspiracy because they could have rectified the injustice, but they chose not to.

"Roland resents them for making him seem like a beggar to get what he believes is rightfully his. He tightens his control over the old ladies and the estate. The aunts thought he was being kind when he made a tradition of inviting them to holiday dinners. He wasn't being kind. He was limiting their contacts.

"He's honest while their attorney is watching. But time is passing. He gets married and has a son. His mother passes. His father is long gone. He's now penniless and he knows he's slated to inherit a fortune. Maybe everything would have played out just as it lay, but Barrington started using hard drugs. Maybe Roland had already made bad investments. Tom Alardi will get a financial rundown on him. But that's not really relevant now. The one who set the crimes in motion was Barry. Parents are prepared to pay for academic expenses. They're never prepared to pay all the medical and legal costs of drug addiction.

"Another universal that you have to look for is a parent's automatic belief in the innocence of his or her child and to place the blame for his crimes on his friends. The worst thing a parent can realize is that he is his child's victim. Barrington believed that he was the only heir of the only heir. He regarded those antiques as his property, too. But when Barry stole a piece, Roland saw it as stealing from Roland. Also, a parent believes his child when he says that he won't do something bad again. He's reformed. To the kid on drugs, it's a joke. The only thing that happens is that the kid now regards his parent as a complete fool for being so gullible."

"So when did Roland form the plan to blame Carla?" Akara asked.

"He may have thought of many schemes and then settled on this one, especially after someone as naive as Carla answered the ad. Carla was perfect because she was a foreigner and didn't appreciate all the niceties of American culture. The rest was easy."

"How do we prevent Carla from being blamed?"

"I went over that up in Philadelphia. We find the friends, the antique furniture, the man who made the custom-made copies, the dog. Beryl and I have to go to the funeral parlor now and openly ask to see those guest books. This morning, she talked to Betty Lou who's willing to testify. But much of what she'll want to say will be considered hearsay. We need other sources. So do a background check and get a list of custom furniture makers and puppy mills or chihuahua breeders. We'll be back in an hour or two."

"I've got a friend who's pulling Barry's sheet," George said. "If he's a hard drug user, you can bet that he got himself in trouble in the past. We'll see where he did his snorting and who his drug connections are."

Beryl and George separately went to the funeral parlor. Beryl went in first.

She presented her credentials to J. Boynton, the owner. "I'm working for attorney Thomas Alardi," she said, "and I've been tasked with getting the names of the kind folks who attended the farewell ceremonies of Daphne and Winifred Buehler. Would it be possible for me to take a quick look at your condolence books?"

"Just don't set off any alarms," Boynton joked. "No doubt you heard the news that someone caused a ruckus here yesterday."

"Ah! Was that your establishment? I caught only the tail end of the news cast." She followed him into the office. "Wisteria!" she gushed. "And it's still blooming this late?"

"They're plastic," he confided. "But don't tell Mr. Alardi that or he might sue me for false advertising."

"I wouldn't worry about that. He told me that when the Good Lord calls him, he wants Boynton to usher him across the Waters."

"He is too kind… and a marvelous attorney. Marvelous."

"Yes, he seems to be a man of quality." She accepted the two guest books and sat at the visitor's desk. A total of fourteen people attended Daphne's ceremony and eleven people attended Winifred's. Why, she wondered, had she not thought to ask how many people were in attendance; or why, for that matter, had Carla not commented on the sparse attendance. Probably Roland had not sent out the announcements or cared to notify anyone other than the civil authorities.

Beryl had nearly finished copying the last of the barely legible names when George entered the showroom ostensibly to inquire about the price and qualities of the caskets on display. He would have kept the owner occupied while Beryl, if necessary, used her iPhone to take photographs of the many pages. As it was, no photography was necessary. She stood up, "Thank you," she said. "I'm finished."

"And I, I do believe, have a possible client waiting in the display room."

As she exited the building she could hear Boynton's effusive greeting and George begin to fumble his way through a request for information about "eternal chambers."

Beryl, imagining him slipping and sliding through all those unctuous phrases, got into her car laughing.

It took George an hour to break away. When he finally opened the door of their motel room he said, "I agreed to think it over. I have to decide if I want my loved one to rest eternally in cherry wood on memory foam and genuine silk satin. I am hereby ordering you to throw my corpse to the sharks… preferably the ones off the Yucatan or Australia's Great Barrier Reef. I'd like to rest eternally there - to be swallowed, digested, and crapped out amid things beautiful." He flopped on the bed. "As if a goddamned stiff cares if the handles on the casket are solid brass."

"Ah," Akara said. "The cycle of life. 'A man may fish with the worm that hath eat of a king, and eat of the fish that hath fed of that worm.' Ya gotta love it."

Beryl showed him the fruits of their afternoon's labor. "I can't even read the writing. The people who signed this book all seem to have Parkinson's. I'm not trying to be funny. It's all written in elderly scratch."

"We'll have to break into the aunts' house and get those cards and letters from the sideboard. We need people to corroborate Carla's statement that she lived with them."

Akara timidly raised his hand. "The house has a security system. Do you want friends of mine to shut off the alarm to their house for an hour or so?"

George looked at him. "You can do that?"

"I can't do it. My attorney wants me to keep my nose clean. It's not a difficult procedure. It's a bookkeeping function. You don't pay your bill, the bookkeeping department orders the service shut off. You pay your bill, the bookkeeping department orders the service to resume. It's a simple job since the system's old... a telephone connection. Anybody in my hackers' club can do it. Tell me when you want to enter the premises."

At 7 p.m. George and Beryl picked the back door lock and entered the aunts' house. All of the cards and letters had been removed from the sideboard and cabinets in the dining room. George did have a list of the eleven faked furniture pieces which Carla had described and located with X's in floor plans she had drawn. They examined each piece of furniture and, after finding absolutely no manufacturer's hallmarks or other identifying imprints, photographed them. The fakes were all well made. It was clear that the omission of manufacturing marks was deliberate.

Akara waited down the street in his Corvette. When they exited the aunts' house, he called his friend to reactivate the alarm system.

THURSDAY, DECEMBER 20, 2012

Sensei sat at Beryl's front office desk, trying to compose the evening's Dharma talk. It was 10 a.m. and he was also hurrying to finish before Lilyanne Smith kept her appointment with him.

Since Sensei knew that she had been assured that both Beryl and George were in Baltimore, he expected her to be dressed casually. Instead she opened the office door and appeared in a business suit. The heart-to-heart talk about babies, in-laws, and criminal fathers did not occur. Lilyanne wanted to discuss Carla Richards, a topic that made Sensei uncomfortable.

Repeatedly, he tried to bring the talk back to the reason they had first begun to speak confidentially: Lilyanne's delayed action to misfortune. He had counseled her as a priest would spiritually guide a congregant. Those talks had occurred nearly a year before when Lilyanne was desperately in need of new ways to view and to solve life's problems. He had begun to help her to understand how so many of her bad decisions were caused by the folly of impetuosity, and that by thinking through any proposed action to its logical conclusion, she would make better decisions. But, stubbornly, she aborted the counseling sessions and had impulsively gone to the Cayman Islands where she set in motion another nearly disastrous sequence of events.

Sensei hoped that as they renewed their talks he would be able to show her how her lack of forethought caused her merely to react to events and not to shape their destiny. To Lilyanne, it was a matter of faith that if one believed that whatever happened was somehow for the best, one had no particular need to influence the future with intelligent planning. Coping well with whatever came to pass seemed a more sensible approach. "Philosophy," she insisted, "far from explaining anything, tends to confuse everything. I've looked into the subject and discovered that if no two philosophers ever agree with each other, what is the point in trying to sort them all out?"

She left the office in an upbeat mood which confused Sensei and left him shrugging at his inability to understand the female mind. He had enough on his male mind trying to contact the woman in *his* life, Sonya Lee. He had allocated an hour of his time for consultation with Lilyanne Smith. She had used only half of it. He picked up his phone and called Hong Kong Customs.

Agent Sonya Lee was not available and no one could give him any information about her whereabouts.

Sensei banged his forehead against Beryl's desk blotter. Two, three, four times. He stood up, slammed the chair back under the desk, locked the office, and returned to the Zen Buddhist temple down the street.

Lilyanne Smith parked her Jaguar at the curb and, carrying a clipboard and looking like an ordinary businesswoman, walked up to George's front door. He had promised her that his home would always be a refuge she could run to in an emergency. As she lifted the gold chain over her head and began to insert the pendant key into the deadbolt she prayed that he had not broken that promise. The lock opened.

She entered the house and stood motionless in the small area of thick stone flooring around the doorway and looked with resentful admiration at the Japanese-styled living room with its tatami platform flooring. She took her high heels off immediately and set them on the stone floor. She had seen the room only briefly some thirteen months before. Civility and George's unrelenting hostility prevented her from seeing it again during the months that she was pregnant. But now, at least in her mind, things could resume... they could just pick up where they left off, before the unhappy adventure in the Cayman Islands. She looked around the room, imagining that it was her room.

The living room, with its low square Japanese table and the orchid blooming in its ikebana arrangement, was perfect. The silk cushions around the table were the precise shade of plum. The scrolls on the wall and the mullioned rice-paper windows and shoji screens enclosed the room protectively. Even the stairway that went to the second storey of the house was not visible from where she stood. She slid open a partition and saw that the stairs had been moved to the entryway that led into the house from the garage. It hurt her to think that George probably used that garage entrance, by-passing the serene living room which he told her he had designed for her.

Carla would probably destroy the elegant simplicity, the serenity. Carla would add coarse and gaudy junk... she'd probably take up the tatami platforms and replace them with wall-to-wall shag carpet... hang painted velvet monstrosities on the walls. No, Lilyanne decided. Even if love and the rights of the beloved had nothing to do with it, artistic sacrilege had to be considered. Carla could not be given the chance to destroy something so exquisite.

She walked back to the closed-off kitchen which served as George's bachelor's pad. She wanted to cry as she looked at his bed in the corner, his recliner and the table beside it, the TV and the kitchen table and chairs. She went into the small bathroom. She opened the door of the shower stall and picked up his bottle of body wash. It was the same as he had used a year ago. She left the stall and opened a bottle of after-shave lotion he kept in a tray on top of the toilet. It was Italian... and expensive. She opened it and the scent had a tactile effect: she felt her face rubbing his cheek. She returned the bottle to the tray and went back into the kitchen. He once kept a Monja Blanca orchid there, but now there were only a couple of unfamiliar ferns in the window. That was all. Suddenly she felt angry. She hadn't come this far to find nothing that represented her. She went to the new staircase that led upstairs and went into his dressing room. He kept duplicate toiletries in his upstairs bathroom for when he showered or soaked his rebuilt knee in a tub of hot water.

She entered his bedroom and looked inside the closet. There at one end were three police uniforms. George hadn't been an active duty police officer in thirteen years. "You sentimental fool!" she said aloud as she lifted a hanger and brought out the navy-blue suit to look at it. "And I bet it still fits." She returned it to the closet and went to a chest of drawers, intending to peek inside them. There were papers and envelopes on top of the dresser, and she stopped to leaf through them. And there she saw a photograph of George and a pretty dark haired woman standing together in front of a sailing ship's mainmast. It wasn't a selfie... someone had taken their picture. The woman was facing forward but he was looking down at her and he was smiling. Lilyanne was stunned. Her heart began to beat faster. Why, they looked like a pair of lovers! She restrained herself from destroying the photograph and returned to the kitchen.

The clipboard she carried contained a yellow legal pad. She clicked her pen and began to write.

"You Rat! You couldn't wait to abandon me. I hadn't eaten a meal in two days and was starved but you couldn't wait to let me swallow a single bite. I called, 'I don't want to look like a scarecrow in a long white dress,' but you were too far down the hall to hear me... scurrying to get away.

And now you think you've replaced me with that woman from the Philippines. Guess again. Tell her I said that she cannot have you because you already belong to somebody else... to me. And I will see us all in hell before I give you to her or anybody else.

Here are two photographs of me. Keep one here in the kitchen and put the other on your dresser and please have the decency to bury that other photograph of you and her. How could you?

Lily."

She left the legal pad on the table with her two photographs propped up against the lamp.

The main conference room at Alardi and Associates had a subdued but politically correct festive look. Poinsettias lined the window sill and a spruce and pine cone centerpiece with red ribbons sat at the center of the huge mahogany table.

Tom Alardi, positioned in the midpoint on the window side of the conference table, polished his new "eye drops" glasses. "I got some kind of foreign body under my lower lid," he explained, "and the eye doc put some drops in my eye and insisted I wear these glasses. He doesn't want me to let too much light in the eye and these glasses are supposed to protect them." He sighed. "There's always something that comes along to spoil things," he said wearily. "Now I'm getting calls at home from some teeny-bopper named Tiffany who insisted on buying me a drink at the Atlanta conference last spring." He looked around, affecting an innocent school-boy look. "How could I say, 'No.' She had the biggest boobs I ever saw." Everyone except his secretary laughed. He made an "Oops!" face and apologized to her. Then he resumed talking about Tiffany, adding, "I don't know how she got my home number."

"Don't tell me we've got a paternity case on our hands!" Jim Guardino, the man Alardi most suspected of being the vicious informant, said. "Will she be calling here?" Again, everyone laughed.

"Well," said Tom with feigned seriousness, "if you should get a call from Tiffany Starkweather, you be sure to put her through to me right away. Don't let me miss out on her stimulating conversation."

As soon as the merriment ceased he began to discuss the Richards' case which was of interest because the possible defendant was not a U.S. citizen. He noted that as soon as possible he'd get Elizabeth Louise Pemberton into the office to take a statement from her. He then realized that he had not brought a recent communication from the State Department regarding foreign defendants, and, claiming that he had to discuss something with his secretary, he asked Guardino to go back to the reference room to see if he could find it in the Richards' file.

Tom Alardi felt slightly disappointed when the man he had suspected of sending the injurious emails returned to the conference room with clean hands. He strained to see through the glasses and began to blubber about eye drops. If the glasses worked, he said to himself, Guardino had not touched the keyboard.

His oldest and most trusted associate, Gus Mellon, stood up to say that there were other documents back in the reference room that had a bearing on the matter being discussed. Before Tom could object, saying that for their purposes at that time, the additional information did not matter, his old associate said, "Give your eyes a rest for a minute. I'm familiar with the file. I'll look." He left the room.

Five minutes later Mellon returned with the documents. Alardi had already removed the cumbersome glasses, claiming that they caused more discomfort than they alleviated. He had placed them on the table beside his left hand and when the documents were handed to him he thoughtfully placed them directly in front of him, as though they were important. The edges of the papers lay against the glasses and suddenly, though one of the lenses, Alardi noticed a strange greenish aura. He rubbed his eyes and put the glasses on and saw the fingerprints of his old associate all over the documents and, as he would later lament, all over the old man's fingertips.

Alardi, confused and fearful, could not continue to chair the meeting. He stammered and, complaining of a sudden feeling of nauseousness, adjourned the meeting. He went directly to the men's room and tried to think. Akara had warned him that more than one of his associates might be responsible for the spurious communications. He wanted to talk to Akara before he did anything else. He went back into the special reference room to see the last email that had been sent. It was one of his own. Whatever had been written last on the computer was now erased.

There was no doubt that Gus Mellon had been the only one to touch the keyboard. Alardi went home and in his wife's arms, he said, "Gus was like a father to me," and he wept, trying to find a reason for the betrayal. "I guess he's getting even with me because I never made him a partner. But most of the other associates are more effective at trial..."

"Yes, darling," his wife consoled him. "You'd have created too much dissension in the group. I guess he felt slighted. That must be it."

He called Akara who advised him to do or say nothing. "You've caught only one. Just bait the trap again. Don't rush to judgment. For all you know, he intends to start his own firm and take some of your people with him. So keep cool and make sure you get them all."

"Gus is coming here for Christmas dinner. Should I say anything?"

"Are you asking me if you need a lawyer? Don't you understand enough to know that you have to act as though you suspect nothing. I'm Mirandizing you. Don't volunteer anything."

"I understand," Alardi said. "This is why lawyers shouldn't represent themselves. I'll keep quiet."

Akara now needed his friends; and with their help he compiled lists of the custom furniture makers and the puppy mills and chihuahua breeders in a fifty-five mile radius around both Hagerstown and Baltimore; and he also had Barry's complete criminal history, including his misadventures at school which never made the official police records. He also had background research files for the aunts, and for Roland's family. He brought the lists to George who was impressed by their thoroughness.

"Oh," he added. "I've also checked with experts in the antiques' business and no Windsor chair has been offered for sale in the last two years. Whoever owns it now has not put it on the market."

Akara drove Beryl home so that she could do some pre-dinner preparation for the Hospice festivities. Sensei would be helping serve dinner, too, and Akara would cover both the temple and the office while Beryl and Sensei were gone. George elected to stay in Baltimore to work with Carla.

Carla would take all the listings for breeders and custom furniture makers on the peninsula where Delaware, Maryland, and Virginia came together, the Delmarva Peninsula. Armed with a chip-reading scanner, a set of photos of substituted furniture pieces, and a list of the addresses of the targeted sites, she headed for the Chesapeake Bay Bridge, and George suddenly found himself alone in Baltimore. He bought large paper maps and laid out road-trip plans for the most efficient geographical approach to the various businesses in northwestern Maryland. For the remainder of the day, he visited the local listings and telephoned various storage facilities to learn the names of the insurance carriers they recommended.

In the evening, Sensei called. George could hear the anguish in his friend's voice. "Still no word?" he asked Sensei. "What does Sonya's boss say?"

"This is crazy! Nobody knows anything. Let's just say that nobody's willing to tell me anything. Who the hell am I? I'm ready to get a flight to Hong Kong to start looking for her myself."

"Perce," George said, "get that idea out of your mind. First, you'd never get a flight at this late date and second, you don't even know what continent she's on. She's no doubt undercover on an assignment. Be patient."

"Do you know how many months it's been since I talked to her? I don't want to hear that 'undercover' shit, G.R.!"

George Roberts Wagner knew that when Sensei referred to him by his initials, he was extremely agitated. "Perce, you've got to be patient."

"She'd have gotten word to me. She would know that I'd be worried sick not hearing from her. What the hell am I gonna do?" He groaned. "Beryl and Akara are back. Beryl's boy called from Arizona. His flight was first delayed and then cancelled. She told him to stay in Phoenix where it's warm and where he could work on his thesis in peace. She's coming up here tonight with Father Willem for dinner with Akara and me. Are you sure you don't want my help? I need to do something, G.R. I'm going nuts sitting here worrying about Sonny. The temple is dead and if Beryl wants to open it for stragglers, she can. Akara is going to head back to you guys tomorrow after I run some errands for the Hospice."

George assured him that he'd be home in another few days. "Christmas is complicating things. With a little luck we'll get somewhere. Carla's over in the Delmarva Peninsula today. I did some investigation but both of us came up with nothing. We'll try again on Friday the 21st and Saturday the 22nd. The pet shops may stay open on Sunday the

23rd; but I don't know about the custom furniture makers. We've got a lot of ground to cover. As soon as I can get free, I'll be home, but you'll be busy at the Hospice. Maybe you can get Father Willem to shoot some pool with you. If not, as soon as I do get back, you and I can play some shuffleboard." It was not a "concretized" plan. Carla, he thought, would have a miserable holiday being alone at such a time. It wouldn't hurt the grand scheme of things if he spent at least part of Christmas Eve or Christmas Day with her. Maybe he'd get her a little gift so she wouldn't feel left out.

George stopped at a jewelry store and bought Carla a gold chain with a simple pearl-drop pendant.

As George wondered what he would have for dinner that Thursday evening, Carla arrived carrying two full-course meals from a quality seafood restaurant. She also brought several bottles of Riesling. She served dinner and then George gave her the necklace. She gasped and looked genuinely pleased. She thanked him while regretting that she hadn't gotten him anything. "It looks pretty on you," he said, "and I'm getting all the gift I need just seeing you not crying for a change."

FRIDAY, DECEMBER 21, 2012

Tom Alardi got out of his car and smelled the early morning air. It had snowed through the night, just enough to clean the air, and whatever pollution had been floating through it was now captured in the inch or two of snow that lay at his feet. Although he dreaded going into his office to feign a happy pre-holiday state of mind, he braced himself and noticed a brown Toyota parked in the visitor's section. Yes, he thought, it might belong to Roland Melbourne who was probably there in some idiotic attempt to manipulate him regarding Carla's case. Alardi had had his fill of manipulative people. If it were Melbourne, he would dispose of him quickly.

He opened the door to his ground floor suite and swung his briefcase as he walked back to his office, nodding good morning to the secretaries and clerks who had arrived on time. As he turned into his waiting room he saw Roland on a chair with a cardboard box on his lap. Melbourne stood up. "You're just the man I came to see," Roland said, "since you seem to be the one who needs convincing."

"I'm representing Carla Richards and if something in that box is calculated to affect the case against her, you're bringing it to the wrong person."

"Oh, I'm on my way to Riordan's office; but I thought you'd like to see what your client has been up to, stealing from me. I didn't count the money she tried to hide, but there are thousands in this can. Wouldn't you like to peek?"

"I'd like to ask my receptionist why she allowed you to come back into my office. If that's evidence you're holding, I'd suggest you take it over to the District Attorney's office. Now, get out of here before I have you thrown out."

That felt good, he decided. He was actually hopeful when his secretary informed him that someone from the medical examiner's office was on the line. The news, however, was not good.

When he hung up he called George to tell him that the medical examiner, having considered the manner in which Winifred Buehler's body had struck the steps, had decided that she had to have been propelled and he therefore ruled her death a homicide.

Worse, he would later learn from Gus Mellon the details of what his earliest visitor had tried to tell him. Roland Melbourne had discovered a canister of cash buried in his back yard. According to Mellon's source, Roland reported that he was at first delighted to have uncovered buried treasure. He had been seeking only pine cones to use for a centerpiece when his eye caught the difference in color and texture of a patch of soil. Naturally, he investigated and when he saw that the container was the metal container of a popular brand of cookies, he realized that he was not likely to find "doubloons or 'crowns, pounds, and guineas,' as the poet says." Hugely disappointed, Roland noted that there seemed to be an excess of fairly new one hundred dollar bills, so much so that he felt compelled to notify the police.

He did not "contaminate" the treasure by handling it. An efficient member of the police department checked the wad of cash for finger prints and Roland was "Shocked! Yes, shocked!" to discover that the prints were those of Carla Richards. (Roland had brought items that the members of his household had used. His Solitaire playing cards. Sybil's recipe book. Barrington's Camper's Guide. And, of course, Carla's employment application.)

Carla was immediately questioned about the cached money. Alardi met her at the police station. She related her story about the Bingo game and the football bets that occasioned the gifts to the church. No such Bingo game had been held. The prosecutor could not help grinning at her naivete about football bettors picking up their moms at a Bingo game when, on that very night, there was a pro-football game being played on TV.

In the event that the fear that Carla would leave the country might outweigh the desire to accumulate evidence in a more thorough manner, Tom Alardi advised her to offer to surrender her passport; but ADA Dave Riordan declined to accept it. He tried to maintain a properly inscrutable expression on his face, but Alardi could tell that the prosecutor was somewhat uncomfortable with such a fortuitous "cookie can" discovery.

He and Carla returned to the motel to discuss the setback. Alardi gave his opinion. "George, they've got the old MMO - Motive, Means, and Opportunity - but I think that they think they got it too easily. I'm encouraged."

He advised Carla, "Enjoy the holidays and attend to your studies. If you leave the country, you will not escape legal consequences. They'll come after you. The pieces that were lost were national treasures and the thought that a foreigner might have disposed of them for a fraction of their worth will find you guilty before you are tried."

Speaking again to George, Alardi reminded him of the essential trouble: "Roland is producing tangible evidence to support the contention that Carla committed the crimes; while we have mostly hearsay evidence. We need to get that friend of Winifred's to come down here for a pre-trial interview as soon as possible. Her testimony is vital, and those old main-line families carry a lot of weight."

George thought the request would carry more "gravitas" if it came from Alardi, himself. He asked the attorney to call Beryl to ask her to visit Betty-Lou Pemberton again and, saying that she was asking per his personal request, explore the possibility of bringing her down to Baltimore to meet with him.

It was noon. The sky was cloudless and the sun easily melted the thin layer of snow. Baltimore's commercial streets were decorated with holly and pine boughs, and Christmas carols were broadcasted on their loud-speaker systems.

Akara bought new clothing to approximate the style George was wearing: a shearling jacket, western hat, and cowboy boots. He secretly always wanted to have that "Marlboro Man" look, and the searching for "a dogie" he joked, gave him the perfect excuse to acquire the look.

Together in the pickup truck, George and Akara, armed with concealed dog chip scanners, headed out for the first puppy mill on the list. They had not expected to find so many people at the owner's home, each wanting to buy a special dog for Christmas. The dogs were held in cages in the back of the property which was completely fenced and impossible to enter. Since it did not seem likely that a chihuahua would be left outside, Akara paid special attention to one garage-type of building at the side of the complex.

"Do you have any chihuahuas?" George asked the owner. "I know you don't sell wholesale but I'll pay top dollar for a chihuahua. I need one of them little dogs and I don't care what it costs."

"You could give me ten grand and I'd still have to tell you that I don't have a chihuahua on the premises."

"Any suggestions as to where I might find one?"

"None."

They had time to visit six pet shops and four custom furniture makers before business hours ended. The result was the same. Nobody knew anything about a chihuahua that could be had for any price whatsoever or, for that matter, copies of antique furniture.

The three met at the motel and, although the double room had been registered to Akara, it was apparent that Carla's presence would complicate the sleeping arrangements, and, leaving everything in place, George stayed in Akara's room and Akara put his things into Beryl's, which fortunately was next door. The three of them went out to have dinner together.

Tom Alardi did not know that ADA Riordan had pulled Barrington Melbourne's "Report of Arrests and Prosecutions" and found drug related charges on it. The RAP sheet also connected Barry to a few thugs in the area; and while he allowed that it was entirely possible that Carla Richards had looted the estate, he was not about to let known criminals pass without being looked at.

Beryl called and made a 1 p.m. appointment to visit the elderly Ms. Pemberton on the following day. With a little luck, she would induce the elderly lady to drive south with her during the week between Christmas and New Years to make a statement to the District Attorney and then Beryl would drive her back to Philadelphia the same day.

SATURDAY, DECEMBER 22, 2012

Early Saturday morning, Akara, George, and Carla met over breakfast and discussed the day's itinerary.

"We'd get more done if we each took a car," Carla said. "We don't need two people to visit a pet shop or a custom furniture maker. A breeder's facility is one thing, but the others we can visit individually." George agreed. Carla returned to the Delmarva Peninsula; and George and Akara, in separate cars, headed west.

At noon, Betty Lou Pemberton returned to her car in the Mall's parking lot. Her arms were filled with Christmas presents, and she had to activate her trunk lock by feeling the remote without even seeing it. As she set a shopping bag down to raise the trunk lid, two short stout men approached her. At first she thought they were going to offer to help her. Just as she put several packages into the trunk, one man asked her if she was Ms. Pemberton. "Why, yes," she said.

Suddenly the other man pulled a stun gun from his pocket and zapped her hand. Fear and the shock paralyzed her. She fell backward into the trunk, sitting open-mouthed in the opening. "You don't know nothing about the Buehler sisters or their antiques. You understand?"

Betty Lou Pemberton could not answer if she had wanted to. She sat in the open trunk of her car and trembled.

"You won't like what happens to you or the rest of your family if you remember anything you heard about them. So just keep your mouth shut." The two men casually walked away.

Little by little she regained her senses and reached into her purse, removed her phone and speed-dialed her daughter. Barely speaking in a coherent way, she told her daughter where she was and to come and get her.

At 1 p.m. as per the appointment, Beryl drove up the Pemberton driveway and parked. A white envelope was conspicuously stuck in between the door and the door jamb beside the Christmas wreathe.

The letter was addressed to her. She opened it and read:

Miss Tilson, Two brutes attacked my mother as she got into her car at the mall. They used a stun gun on her and said that she should forget everything she discussed with both Buehler women. They asked, "Do you understand?" She was paralyzed momentarily, but she understood very well, indeed.

My mother was terrified and in considerable pain. She has burns on her hand from the electrical contact points. I have removed her to a place that is and shall remain unknown to you, and I beg you not to pursue the matter. I do not think you would expect her to risk her life over the loss of property regardless of its historical significance. She repeatedly advised the Buehler sisters to give the pieces to a museum where they would be protected. It was foolish for them to retain such items in their home. My mother should not have to pay for their foolishness.

Elizabeth Pemberton Borden

12/22/12

Beryl returned to her car and called George. "I'm going to drive down to Baltimore and give this letter to Tom Alardi," she said. "I think he may want to discuss the situation at a pre-trial conference. The introduction of these thugs into the crime is going to cast a whole new light on the case. There undoubtedly are now federal considerations."

It was a setback for which George was not prepared. He agreed with Beryl and called Tom Alardi to give him the gist of the letter that she was en route to deliver.

Alardi expressed alarm at the introduction of this new violence and the character of the perpetrators. "This isn't kid stuff anymore; but without the witness or her daughter here to testify about the incident at the Mall or the authenticity of the letter, it's not going to be admissible. I've requested a pre-trial conference with ADA David Riordan who seems oddly sympathetic to the defendant.

"Nevertheless, on the basis of evidence thus far adduced, it looks to me as if his office is going forward with charging Carla Richards. Incidentally, I was contacted by the Philippine consul's office. They're sending an observer to the conference which I learned last night has tentatively been scheduled for 10 a.m. on Thursday, 12/27/12, in Judge Tom O'Donnel's chambers. I'm trying to get somebody down here from Washington County - that's where Hagerstown is located."

"What's bothering me," George said, "is how the thugs knew that Betty-Lou Pemberton had agreed to testify for Carla. Roland may have known where she lived and that his aunt spoke to her a month ago, but nobody knew that Beryl had got her to agree to come to Baltimore."

Alardi felt a sickening tug in his stomach. "Part of the problem I was having and discussed with Dr. Chatree was that a pernicious leak was occurring in my office. Yes, it could have come from elsewhere; but for now, I won't continue to inform my staff of any developments in the case. I'll get another disposable phone and give you the number, and please don't convey any information to me until Chatree and I can solve my problem. Let's all be circumspect in our communications."

Akara had a question. "Why did they just stun the old lady? She can still talk. Why didn't they just silence her completely... you know, kill her outright?"

Tom Alardi heard the question. "Do you want to field this, George, or should I?"

"I'll do it. First of all she's an important witness. They can easily force her to say that Winifred told her that Carla lived with Roland and make

Carla look even more guilty by making nasty little remarks. Remember! Betty-Lou wasn't Winifred's only friend. So even if they killed Betty-Lou, there could be many others who would reveal that Winifred said that Carla lived with the aunts. So scaring her into silence is the smart thing to do. Later, if they need her, they'll scare her into perjury."

"Oh," Akara said. "I get it."

The attorney heard the explanation. "He learns fast. Hang onto that kid."

George returned to the lists. "It's even more important now that we find that furniture maker and the dog."

"The furniture maker is your best bet," Alardi said. "For all you know they destroyed the dog. They can't so easily do away with a man who's in business making furniture. So concentrate on him."

"We'll get right on with searching for him," George said.

"We're running out of time," Alardi said. "Once they arrest Carla, the gauntlet will be thrown down and it will be a long and expensive fight. Keep searching." He checked the time. "I'll drive to the motel now to get the letter. I'll probably get there at the same time Beryl does." He ended the call.

Akara disagreed about foregoing investigations into the dog. "I'm not saying that the guy who made the furniture copies isn't important, but even if we find him, he can lie and we'll just keep looking. He made sure he didn't put his hallmark seared into the pieces as they usually do, so he knows the jobs were to be kept secret. I think the greed of the Melbourne family is such that they'd never destroy a dog they could probably get an easy thousand for, bad leg or not. Bonbon was a pedigree animal. And when we get a scanner reading, we know it's the truth."

Carla, who had stayed overnight at the motel, sought cooperation. "Akara," she said, "neither of us is licensed. We just can't go off on our own. George and Beryl are operating under Mr. Alardi's aegis."

In the midst of this discussion Beryl arrived. Akara showed her the classified ads and insisted that the smart thing to do was call them first. "There are half a dozen chihuahuas for sale by private dog owners. And I've got a list of all the registered chihuahua owners."

Tom Alardi also arrived and entered the discussion. "We would do better," he countered, "if you had a list of all the licensed furniture makers!"

"I do have it," Akara said quietly. "I printed it out on the printer they keep in the lobby." He handed Alardi a copy of the list of furniture makers.

"Jesus!" Alardi said, looking over George's shoulder at the list. "We're gonna need more investigators."

"We can investigate the dogs for sale!" Beryl argued. "Aside from big newspapers, inside every supermarket there are a bunch of small local papers - mostly real estate but a lot of 'garage sale' type ads. Dogs are often listed lost, found, or for sale. The people with chihuahuas are the people who know the gossip about chihuahua sales."

"Forget the goddamned dog," Alardi snapped. "We have no time to waste going to private homes to look at their puppies."

Beryl held up a hand. "No. No. No. Akara's right. What's the most likely place to dump a valuable dog? With a small-time breeder. They always have the pedigree papers from dead dogs. Bonbon is valuable. We can do this over the phone. All of you, sit down and be quiet." She turned to Carla. "Which of Bonbon's legs was damaged?"

"Her left rear leg."

Alardi did not know quite how to respond. He did not want to antagonize his investigators, but he did want to assert his leadership. The result was a red-faced stuttering objection.

Beryl called the first number. "I see you have chihuahuas for sale," she said sweetly. "I'm wondering if you might have heard of a lame female chihuahua who was taken from us. We're offering a $2000 reward, no questions asked. I have a granddaughter who was born with a deformed left leg. She's unable to play with other kids because she also has a lung problem. She identified with the dog because of the similar leg problem. It was the only thing that kept her active and happy... just playing with it. But," Beryl gasped and let her voice weep, " that wonderful dog was just whisked away by some stranger. We are disconsolate. If you have the dog or can help me to find it, I'll reward you in cash, no questions whatsoever... plus paying the current owner."

The lady shared some gossip with her. "The most likely place to get paid for a stolen chihuahua was a place near the West Virginia border... just southwest of Hagerstown. 'Dog Ranch' or something it's called." Beryl made a note and thanked her. She also left several contact phone numbers.

Alardi calmed down. "*Ancora imparo,*" he whispered. Akara laughed.

George grinned. "People think I keep her around because she's a good cook. Even removes the cardboard box! That's a great skill, but this... this ability to lie automatically! Can't put a price on talent like that!" He began to laugh as Beryl threw a shoe at him.

As Beryl prepared to call the next number, she said, "We don't require an audience. Why don't you guys get moving on your furniture makers. I'll call you if I learn anything."

Tom Alardi looked at the list. "I'm going home. The last two on this list are on are on my way. I'll stop and check them out myself." He turned to Akara. "Can you step outside with me for a moment?"

Akara went outside to confer with his attorney. Tom Alardi was in a helpless state of mind. "I'm losing my effectiveness in my office because I can't think straight. I don't want my clients to suffer because I'm distracted. If I screw up, people could go to prison. Can't you think of a low-tech way to find out who else could be sabotaging me?"

"Personally, I'd draft an iron-clad non-compete clause and ask them all to sign it... including your secretaries and clerks."

"Yes! I could do that!" Alardi exclaimed.

"But get another outside lawyer to do it. Don't trust yourself."

"And what would a high-tech solution be?"

"Provide $20K to a non-regulation hacking club along with a complete list of associates and their family members - middle names, ages, and addresses - so that the Local Usage Details of their phone conversations over the last few months can be analyzed and cross referenced. There will be calls to commercial real estate firms... interior decorators... sign makers... stationery suppliers... It depends on how far along their break-away project has gotten."

"And where do I send the list and the 20K?"

"You don't send anything anywhere. Start low-tech. Just have the non-compete clause drawn up and then call me with the results."

Carla watched Tom leave. She picked up the list and the photographs and headed for the Chesapeake Bay Bridge and the businesses listed on the Delmarva Peninsula. Beryl took the list and photographs to canvass the small breeders in and around Baltimore.

Akara and George divided the list, and in separate vehicles left to check out the puppy mill operations that were located in the western part of the state. Hagerstown also fell in that area, but they decided not to venture into West Virginia as per the suggestion of the lady Beryl had spoken to regarding the advertisement. Female gossip, George decided, was not exactly persuasive.

At the end of the business day they had come up with nothing. They headed back. Beryl and Carla, too, had not gained a single lead.

"Tomorrow is Sunday," George announced over a pizza dinner. "I don't know about the guys who make furniture, but the Christmas rush for presents will keep the pet shops and dog breeders open."

Beryl and Akara went next door to what technically was George's room, and George and Carla stayed in Akara's original room. Everyone needed to get a good night's sleep.

SUNDAY, DECEMBER 23, 2012

Beryl, Carla, George and Akara met again Sunday morning and, over breakfast at a coffee shop, planned their routes for the day. Once again Carla headed for the other side of Chesapeake Bay, Beryl stayed in the area, and George and Akara headed west.

By lunch time no one had had any luck. They communicated their failures by cellphone and laid out the afternoon's targets.

Akara had made a note alongside the name of a mysterious breeder in West Virginia: "specializes in chihuahuas." He explained, "When breeders advertise they usually say, 'Wholesale only,' since they don't want to be seen as competition for the pet shops that buy their dogs. This one says nothing, not even that he's a breeder. It's probably the one that Beryl was told about."

"How the hell did you find it?" George asked.

"The owner had been cited for violating animal protection laws four years ago."

George shook his head. "Amazing. There are other promising leads here in these small Hagerstown supermarket papers. Let's phone them and then hit a couple puppy mills, including this one that you listed as a chihuahua specialist. We'll have to cross the Potomac River, here." He drew a line on the map. "Let's call on that lawbreaker breeder at night. It's holiday party time and maybe he'll be celebrating."

They split up and agreed to meet back in the Waffle House next to the motel at 6 p.m.

Akara parked his car under an overhead lamp in a little used corner of the motel parking lot. He got into George's pickup and together they drove into West Virginia.

It was dark but cloudless, and the gibbous moon cast an eerie light on the patches of snow that glinted on the field. In the distance they could see a single overhead light fixture... a bulb, protected with a metal umbrella disk, hung over a sign. They could smell the "Doggie Ranch" and hear the whimpering and howling of the animals long before they could read the sign.

"This must be the place," George said, and Akara, sitting in the pickup's passenger seat, responded, "I hope you intend to bring your gun."

George unlocked the glove compartment and took out his Colt. "Don't leave home without it... not when you live around here." He put the weapon in the left pocket of his shearling jacket.

A single tree marked the edge of the road. "Let's park there," Akara said.

George estimated the kennels to be an uphill hundred meters back from the road. "Is there no side road that leads back up there?" he asked, stopping the truck in the middle of the road and turning off the headlights.

Akara opened the door and stood on the floor, holding on to the cab's roof. "Sure, if you want to drive alongside the house." He swung back into his seat.

George pulled over to the side of the road and parked beneath the barren tree. They got out and stepped onto the crunching slush of frozen snow at the roadside. Outside the kennel smell was worse.

"Let's park on the other side of the house," Akara suggested. "We may be downwind now and the stench might not be so bad on the other side."

"No," George said. "I can't tell which way the wind's blowing... or if it's even blowing at all. But if this is the downwind direction, we're ok.

So far we haven't gotten any special notice. If we move to the other side, their guard dogs may pick up our scent."

"Gotcha'," Akara said.

The house was dark although a faintly flickering light suggested that someone inside was watching television. They walked together, avoiding the patches of crusted snow. The barking grew louder. A partially opened gate presented an opening in the chain link fence that surrounded the compound. They squeezed through and entered the rear of the property.

Most of the cages were under a corrugated aluminum roof that prevented snow from falling on them, but they were otherwise exposed to the cold. Burlap sacks and old blankets lay bunched inside the cages, most of which had chicken-wire floors that allowed feces to fall through. "A chihuahua doesn't stand a snowball's chance in hell of surviving out here," George noted.

While patches of snow still lay on the top of the aluminum roofs, one shed that was closed on all sides had no snow on the roof. "That's probably where they keep the really small dogs," Akara said. "Let's check it out."

As they moved towards the shed they unknowingly tripped an electronic beam which opened a pen in which two rottweilers were housed. Instantly the dogs bolted towards George and Akara. George was closer and both dogs jumped on him, knocking him down. The first dog sank his teeth into George's thigh while the second bit down hard on his left shoulder pad, shaking his head so forcefully it nearly succeeded in pulling the jacket off. Akara, remembering that the Colt was in George's left pocket, pulled his glove off with his teeth as he lunged on top of the second dog, covering its body and trying to hold its head in a head-lock with his left arm. He reached into the pocket, withdrew the gun, and fired directly into the dog's head. Bone, gore, and blood sprayed into the air, nearly blinding Akara, who wiped his eyes, squinted, and pressed the muzzle of the gun into the chest of the dog that had George's flesh in his mouth. He fired and the dog released his jaws and arched it back, writhing in pain. The house's lights went on as Akara pulled George to his feet and supported him as they tried to escape.

The wounded dog squealed and yelped in pain and retreated to its owner who emerged from the house carrying a shotgun. The man cursed and shouted at the two intruders. Akara steered George through the gate and nearly dragged him, stumbling downhill towards the road.

The owner could not fire his weapon for so long as there were cages between him and the intruders. As George and Akara neared the truck the owner was finally able to fire, and pellets fell like a Perseid shower around them. Akara opened the passenger door and pushed George up into the seat. He ran around to the driver's side and as he got behind the wheel George handed him the ignition key. Instinctively, Akara's left foot began stomping on the floor. "Where's the fucking clutch?" he hissed and George shouted, "It's an automatic!" But Akara had already figured that out and dropped the shift into drive. By the time the owner reached the road, everything that was behind the pickup truck had disappeared in the frosty exhaust of eight determined cylinders.

"Where do you want me to take you? There's a town called Martinsburg up ahead or do you want to go back to Hagerstown?"

"Drive straight back to Baltimore."

"Bullshit! You've been bitten bad. I'm taking you into Hagerstown. Don't argue."

"Ok. Go as fast as you can. I've got a tourniquet... my belt... I can put on the bite. And I've got my credentials with me if they stop us for speeding. Jesus this hurts."

"I hated to kill those dogs. They were just doin' their job."

"Yeah," George snapped, "Like Nazi concentration camp guards. I'd like to come back and plug the son of a bitch who owns the place."

"Won't he say we were trespassing?"

"Akara, if you come upon a man raping a child, when you stop him, he can't complain that you've interfered with his love making."

"The guy probably has a license... he's legal."

"Then let the people who licensed him answer for their negligence - which usually means bribery. No honorable citizen of West Virginia would knowingly tolerate the conditions we saw."

At Memorial Hospital in Hagerstown, George was treated for a severe dog bite. Asked to tell the location of the dog so that the authorities could pick it up and also determine if the animal had been vaccinated for rabies, George hesitated, and Akara said, "It was on the road to Hagerstown on the other side of the Potomac. We had to change a tire and he went to the side of the road to relieve himself, and the dog jumped out of the bushes. He's a retired police investigator and while he wrestled with the dog I was able to get his gun and shoot the animal. I'm not familiar with the area so I can't be more specific than that." Akara's Brazilian passport and his Pennsylvania driver's license and the pickup's registration gave credence to his story. "The dog had a collar and metal disks attached to it."

While they worked on George, Akara called Beryl. She and Carla were together in her motel room, waiting for news from them. "Is it bad?" Beryl asked.

"Bad, but they're not keeping him so I guess the answer is 'Painful but curable.'"

"Have you eaten?" Beryl asked.

"No," Akara said.

"Then we'll go out and find a fast food joint that's still open."

"Get fried chicken if you can... and cole slaw."

George also received a rabies vaccination, antibiotics, and a tetanus shot. When his pants were cut off, the doctors saw his scarred knee. "You've had a lot of surgery," one said, giving him an old pair of scrub pants to wear.

"Yeah," said George, "so you'll have to go easy on the painkillers. I spent a year in rehab. You should see my shoulder."

"Which one? Line of duty wound?"

"Right shoulder... and yes."

The doctor opened George's snap-closed cowboy shirt and looked at the remedial work done on his brachial plexus. "Only a year in rehab?" he said.

"Just as we put you in a wheel chair to take you out of here, I'll give you a shot for your pain. He documented George's wound with his phone camera. If your car is right outside, you'll be in it before you feel it. And this guy here looks like he could handle you from there on in. I'll also write you a script for some Percocet. Let's not be too heroic," he said.

He asked Akara to return the next day. "I'll be on again tomorrow night at 7 p.m. Bring him back after then and I'll have a look at him. If you're not in town, take him to an ER wherever you are. That's a bad bite."

"Where's your Corvette?" Beryl asked.

"Jesus! My car! It's about sixty miles from here in front of a motel."

"A motel in which you have a room?"

"No. I just parked it there when George and I met to go to into West Virginia."

"Show me on a map." Akara struggled to remember and finally had to raise Google's detailed image on his iPad before he found the place. The distance was at least a hundred miles. "You don't want to leave your car there overnight. It might be towed away. Come on. I just gassed up the Explorer. We'll go get it. Carla is staying with George."

MONDAY, DECEMBER 24, 2012

It was 3 a.m. by the time Akara and Beryl returned with the completely undamaged Corvette. They looked into George's room and saw that he and Carla were both asleep. The television was on. They did not cross the room to turn it off.

"Let's get to sleep," Beryl said. "You've got your own bed in my room."

Akara could barely keep his eyes open. "I could sleep on subway tracks I'm so goddamned tired."

Carla Richards would have termed it "incorrect" to say that she awakened at 5 a.m. Awaken suggests the state that follows sleep; and the fitful passing in and out of a series of dreamy actions that vaguely corresponded to the back to back episodes of *Law and Order* she had begun to watch at midnight could not be called sleep. She took a cold shower, dressed, and took an ice bucket, filled it with soapy water and, carrying a bunch of paper towels, went out to wash the seat of George's pickup.

She knocked on Beryl's door. Akara answered, "You're up early."

"Couldn't sleep and it's George's time for medication. Give me all your dirty laundry - the laundry room in the motel is empty. I can get it done quickly. And when the stores are open I'll buy him new jeans, shirt, and jacket. What about you? Need anything?"

Akara handed her a pile of dirty clothes. "These are fine if they come clean. But I could use another jacket. I'd never be able to get it cleaned." He went to his wallet. "Let me give you some money."

She refused it. "I can access an ATM. Give me the jacket so I get the right size." She looked at Beryl who had not moved an inch since Carla entered the room. "I'll let her do her own laundry," she whispered. "She can't have much." She returned to George's room.

George was stirring. His leg and his hip hurt. "Between the fangs and the needles, I'm wounded... badly," he said.

Carla gave him his medication for pain and his antibiotics. "Do you want me to help you to the bathroom or do you want me to get Akara? He's awake. He and Beryl got his Corvette last night. I saw it outside."

"Yes. Get Akara. I can't walk. And my leg is killing me."

Carla brought Akara to the room and then left to do the laundry. When that chore was finally done, she left to go to the stores that were open earlier than usual because of the Christmas season.

Cecelia Smith was prepared to dislike the Haffners. "Their DNA-collecting spy wanted to engage a limousine to bring them here from the airport. I told Erica that at this time of year airport traffic was horrendous and there was no point in making it worse with one of those god-awful hearses. I'd come with our driver in the family car to pick them up. They'll probably wear disguises so that they won't be recognized getting into the back seat of a ordinary four-door Jaguar."

The Lufthansa 777 landed on time and Erica and Hans Haffner, as passengers in first class, emerged first from the jetway. Cecelia waved her arm and called them by their first names - a rudeness not easily forgiven in Austrian circles.

A porter picked up their luggage from the carousel, and by cellphone, Cecelia informed her driver who was parked in the temporary parking lot that they were now headed for the arrival platform and that he should come immediately.

As they settled into the car and began the drive to Tarleton House, Cecelia Smith explained the ground rules as though she were a referee at a prize fight. "You know that there's to be no discussion of Eric. My daughter does not know if he is dead or alive or where he might be in either case. You have your own resources and I'm sure that if you wanted to find him at any time during the last twenty years, you could have."

"We have found him and observed his life," Erica Haffner assured Cecelia Smith. "From time to time we've hired an investigator to send us photographs of him. To pick up his monthly check he had to make an appearance at one post office or another. He has been in unsavory company for twenty years."

"When did you last see him... face to face?" Cecelia asked.

"In 1992. He had been dismissed from his school in Vienna and we sent him to an academy in Lyon that was said to specialize in recalcitrant young men. It was a mistake. We should have investigated more. Instead we took the word of well-meaning but utterly unqualified advisors. He entered the school as a confused boy. He left it as a clear thinking criminal. But that, of course, is just my opinion. To my knowledge he has not been in prison anywhere."

"My wife and I," Hans Haffner managed to enunciate,"don't discuss the people with whom he became family."

"Good," said Cecelia. "Then we shall get along famously. We do not discuss them either."

Lilyanne was gracious. She did not, however, get close enough to them to offer each cheek in salutation. She extended her right hand and said, simply, "Welcome to our home." She held up her left hand, slightly pointing an index finger, and Sanford appeared to order the houseboy to take their luggage to the chosen guest room. "You've come all this distance to see Baby Eric," she said pleasantly, "and I will not delay the completion of your mission." She raised her left hand again, and Sanford asked the nanny to bring the baby into the room.

The baby gurgled and seemed to be smiling as the nanny placed him in Madame Haffner's arms. She cooed over the baby and to Cecelia and Everett's surprise asked if it were permissible to undo the baby's diaper to see his genitals. Everyone said, "Ah!" and Everett looked at Hans Haffner and said, "Well Hans, which one of us does he take after?" Everyone laughed. The ice was not only broken. It had melted. And everyone finally was on a first name basis.

"I've engaged a professional photographer who will come and take your photographs with the baby if you should so desire," Everett said.

The photographer was summoned and an endless series of photographs in all possible permutations was taken, including placing an old antique Christmas ornament - which Eric would be certain to remember - in the child's lap. The photographer left and the tree decoration was memorialized with only personal photographic equipment.

Hans asked if they should take one of the baby naked. As if no other infant ever was able to cling to the index fingers of an adult, their special superman grandson held onto Hans' fingers long enough for the photographer to take several photos of the naked hero.

Dinner was served in the closed patio which was decorated with dozens of orchids from their greenhouse. The Haffners had already learned that The Smiths of Tarleton House were famous for their orchids.

At least a thousand times during the next two days, Lilyanne Smith would remember Eric's prediction. "You'll wait until you are presented as a madonna and then you tell the world that your child is Satan's Spawn." She couldn't remember his exact words, but that was close enough.

Had SS not stood for Schutzstaffel she might have told the grandparents that she nicknamed him per his father's suggestion as SS. Satan's Spawn. As it was she would make raspberries on his belly and call him her Scrumptious Son.

It was nearly noon before everyone assembled in George's room. "We've got two days 'till the pre-trial hearing, and we've got nothing," George announced.

"We don't need three people to look after you," Beryl chided. "Akara and I can continue the search."

George tried to appear to be serious. "There are other breeders who specialize in chihuahuas," George said. "Why not give them *their* chance to take a shot *at you?* Fair's fair."

"We also need to get the names of the aunts' friends since Betty-Lou Pemberton is no longer a source of information," Beryl announced. "Our list of people who would gain from the loss of her testimony has gotten longer. Now it's not just Roland and his family, but all of Barry's creditors - which is probably a very long list."

"We have to find more friends and connections," George insisted. "And Barry's dealings may be documented. Where would those records be?"

"In Roland's basement," Carla said. "He has a row of file cabinets for his own records and a row for the aunts. The files aren't locked but the house is wired for an alarm - the same system that the aunts have."

"I don't know how well I'll be able to walk, but somehow we've got to get into their basement and get to those files. That son of a bitch thinks he's way ahead of us. So far he is." His pain medication was winning the battle for his consciousness and he began to drift into sleep.

"What about locating Bonbon in those puppy mills and breeders in the western part of the state?" Carla asked. "If you don't mind lying here alone, Akara and I can go out to that puppy mill where you were bitten. The surviving dog's got Akara's scent. If he shows up there that dog will go wild. I'll go in my car. Akara can keep his distance in the pickup. We can continue to work on the lists. A disreputable puppy mill is just the sort of place Roland would use. Beryl can work the local lists of custom furniture makers to keep Tom Alardi happy."

"Go ahead," George mumbled. "When you get back, we can go see that doc again." He closed his eyes and seemed to be asleep before he finished speaking.

In the pickup, Akara, illegally armed, followed Carla. He waited at what he thought was a safely unrecognizable distance on the "Doggie Ranch" road.

With her microchip scanner in her tote bag, she approached the owner's residence and knocked gently on the door.

"Yes?" a man answered the knock.

"Please forgive me if I've disturbed you, but in town I was told that you might have a chihuahua dog for sale out here."

"You were told wrong. I ain't got one." He looked out at the road and saw the dark colored pickup. "That your pickup?"

"No. But I think it might have followed me out here. I don't know who it is. Hmmm. Well, do you happen to know of anyone who might have one of those dogs? I'll pay any price... no price is too high... to get a chihuahua dog for a sick child for Christmas."

"You with those two fellas who was going around town lookin' for a chihuahua?" He showed her his shotgun. "You with them two guys who shot my dogs?"

"No!" Carla tried to look both confused and irate. "I haven't been with any fellas... not ones who shot your dogs or ones who didn't. Well! A Merry Christmas to you and I guess that's all I can say." She turned and with her spine tingling with fear that she'd be shot in the back, she left his porch and walked to her car.

As she drove away, she could see the man observe Akara in the pickup and then to write down his license number as he passed. She went another mile and pulled over. Akara parked behind her.

As they both stood on the road, she explained that the owner might notify the police that a truck that probably belonged to the intruders had just passed. "There's likely to be a roadblock up ahead. Give me George's gun. I'll put it on top of my head, inside my parka hood."

Akara gave her the gun which she securely placed inside her hood.

Sure enough, before they had gone another couple of miles, a highway patrol officer pulled them over and searched Akara's car. Carla, whose car was registered in Maryland, pretended that she did not know the person who drove the Pennsylvania licensed vehicle. The officer gave a cursory look inside her car, and then signaled them both to continue.

They traveled back towards Hagerstown and stopped to have lunch. Carla left her car parked outside and got into the pickup, and together they drove to the next breeder on the list, Grieg's Small Dogs near Hagerstown. Mr. Grieg seemed to be harassed by the demands of Christmas. Carla shortened her pitch. "We're lookin' to buy a chihuahua dog. Got one or know where we can get one?"

"My wife breeds Burmese cats. You wanna cat, I can sell you one. But dogs? We sell only wholesale. I sometimes buy papered dogs from owners - to keep the breed healthy - but I don't sell 'em. I'd be competing with my own customers. But not chihuahuas. Whelpin' 'em's a nightmare."

"We had wanted to buy a chihuahua to replace one that was lost," Akara said. "It had a malformed left hind leg."

"Why didn't ya say so? I had a kid here a month or so back, wanting to sell me a lame one for a thousand dollars. I told him to get the hell off my property."

The remark startled Akara. "Because he wanted to sell you a lame chihuahua?"

"No. Cause he gives me a song and dance about having to sell his dog to buy his grandmother an airplane ticket so she can come home for Christmas. He's got the dog all wrapped up in a blanket. Cute little face. My wife has a friend that breeds 'em. I says, 'You got papers for this dog?' As I take her from him to look at her and right away I see that she's been cut around her withers. He had hacked the chip right outta 'er.

"'No,' he says, 'but maybe you got papers lying around from a bitch that died. Can't you just use them on her? Who's gonna know?'

"I said, 'If you ain't off my property in two minutes, I'm callin' the cops.'"

"Any idea where he might have taken her?" Carla asked.

"There's a bunch of us out this way. Some are specialty breeders that also train workin' dogs. A few handle only small breeds, but nobody I know who would touch a dog without papers. There's DNA today. You can prove a bloodline. But I don't think he knows that. Try some of the others. Maybe they'd give him a few bucks for the dog because they felt sorry for it. Somethin' was wrong with that kid." Mr. Grieg pointed to his head. "Somethin' funny."

Akara let Carla drive as he consulted the Google images on his iPad. They were directed onto a country road where the fallen leaves, frozen by the sunless air, stuck up like jagged pieces of glass through the roadside snowbanks. The tall, evergreen pines broke the monotony and they drove slowly on the winding trail that dipped down into frozen creeks and rivulets. Sparrows that never headed south - "Little Zen Nuns" Akara called them since they were so drab compared to the birds of Thailand and Brazil - hopped along the roadway looking for anything edible. Sparrows, like nuns, were permitted no food preferences.

When they arrived at the "Minit Men Breeders" establishment, they were met at the gate by two heavily armed paramilitary guards who wore boots and camouflage fatigues. They came to attention as Carla approached.

Carla noticed immediately that the left ear lobe of one of the men had recently been lacerated and scratched. "I'll do the talking," she said. She opened the driver's side door and walked up to them.

"I hope I've got the right place," she said. "I'm looking to buy a chihuahua, but since I'm also a doctor, I'm also looking at that tear in your ear lobe. Sir, you do not want to let your ear get infected. Was that a dog bite?"

"It'll heal," he said.

"Of course it will. But unless it's stitched, it will heal ugly. Stitched, it will barely be noticeable. And you need tetanus and rabies shots."

"I just had shots and our dogs are all vaccinated. And I ain't goin' into any hospital to get it stitched. You're a doctor. You wanna stitch it?"

"Fortunately, there are very few nerve endings in the ear lobe. So while I have nothing technical to suture it with, I can make a go of it with a needle and thread and alcohol and a bandage."

The wounded man turned to the other guard. "Call the house and have Vivian bring down a needle and thread and some alcohol and a box of Band-aids."

The guard called the house and relayed the message.

Carla called, "Ask her if she's got a lame chihuahua up there, and some ice cubes to numb the area."

The guard repeated the request for ice cubes and snapped the phone shut. "We don't handle nothing but big guard dogs. A chihuahua ain't even fit for them to practice on."

The thought that Bonbon might be thrown to a fighting dog for "practice" was disconcerting. Carla dismissed the thought from her mind and prepared herself to sew the man's ear lobe in a professional manner. George kept a roll of paper towels and an aerosol can of window cleaner in the pickup. She had Akara spray her hands and then she wiped them with the paper towels.

Vivian came down the driveway to the gate. She handed Carla the supplies and said, "You the lady lookin' for a lame chihuahua?"

Carla looked up. "Yes. Yes, I am. Do you know of one?" She held the ice to the man's earlobe and then began to sew the torn parts together.

"No, we don't deal with those fancy dogs. But I got an idea you could try. In Hagerstown there's a hospital for kids with bone problems... a lot of crippled kids. Our group has a ladies' auxiliary, and one of the ladies works three afternoons a week at the hospital. Now... she says whenever somebody donates a crippled dog or cat to the animal shelter... a friendly animal... they call the hospital people to see if they want it. If it's friendly, they clean it up and check it out to make sure it's housebroken and then they take it for the kids to play with. The kids feed 'em and try to take them for walks. Sometimes they let the family take it home when the kid goes home. Those animals really help the kids to recover. So I was thinkin' maybe you could look there."

"That's a wonderful lead," Carla said as she finished sewing the man's ear. "If you feel the slightest soreness or redness, get to the hospital. They'll give you some antibiotics. Otherwise, get the stitches taken out in about 5 days." She showed Vivian how to remove the sutures with a cuticle scissors and tweezers.

Vivian took Carla's phone number. "I'll call our member. The animal rights people are trouble, so I have to be careful. I'll tell her what you're lookin' for and she can call you direct. We take precautions around here."

Carla thanked her profusely and got into the pickup. "I'll wait to hear from your friend... and God bless you all. Merry Christmas!"

The guards waved goodbye holding up their AK-47s.

At the motel, Beryl took George to a local hospital to have his wounds checked. He was healing nicely but he'd be unable to walk normally for another week. Hospital policy required that Beryl wheel George in and out of the building in a wheel chair. He griped the entire time. "My good leg... that goddamned dog had to bite my good leg. I'm goin' back there and I better find two goddamned crosses on his lawn."

"Or what?" Beryl said, "You'll kick the mutt that's still alive? You're supposed to rest. Watch TV. Maybe there'll be some *Lassie* re-runs on."

Akara and Carla knew that Beryl would be leaving before noon to return to Philadelphia. They did not want to leave George alone, but there were still too many names of breeders and furniture makers on the list. Akara had gotten a picture array of old "step up" delivery trucks and Carla had pointed to the photo of a 1961 Ford P-400 as the one that looked most like the one that picked up the antique pieces and delivered the new ones. He had a list of all current owners of the 1961 Ford - of which there were only a few - and of trucks that were old but similarly designed. He cross-referenced the list with custom cabinet and furniture makers. "We've got six in a 75 mile radius," he announced. "While we're waiting to hear from the Ladies Auxiliary we can run these leads down."

They visited three custom furniture makers. Two had their vehicles parked alongside their shops. Carla knew immediately that these were not the trucks. They did not even get out of the pickup to inquire further. The third shop was closed for the day but there was a garage affixed to the side of the shop. Akara parked and Carla went to the glass inserts at the top of the garage door and peeked inside. Two trucks were there but neither was the one that had made the deliveries. Dejected, she returned to the pickup just as her phone was ringing. Vivian's friend was calling.

"My name's Dee Dee Marquis. I'm with the Minit Men Ladies' Auxiliary. Vivian tells me that you're a good gal and I should help you all I can. The hospital got word a week or so ago that a chihuahua was brought into the shelter. The dog was in pretty bad shape with an infection when Animal Control picked it up but it's recovering now. I'm sorry to say that already a dozen people have claimed it, saying that she's their dog. When the ten day holding period is over, the shelter staff will have to make a decision."

"How can people claim a dog that isn't theirs? I mean... the dog can't belong to two different families. And since the owner hasn't claimed it—"

"Doctor Richards, you'd be surprised. Some'll come in with beef blood on their sleeves and lapels. You'd be surprised how fast a strange dog will jump up into their arms. Does your phone have video capability?"

"No, but I'm with someone who does have it." She gave Dee Dee Marquis Akara's number.

"I asked the shelter to give me a printout of the picture they took of the dog. It's a grainy picture that will not photograph well, but I can show you the picture on screen if that will help. It also would be nice to talk to you in person."

The phone call was disconnected and in another minute on Akara's iPad she watched Dee Dee holding a letter-sized printout of the dog's photo.

Akara had no way of knowing anything about the appearance of the dog, but the young woman who held the dog, Dee Dee Marquis, was a very winsome blonde whose hair was coiffed in a fetching Prince Valiant kind of "page boy" style and whose smile, he thought, was "irresistible."

"My God!" Carla said. "That looks like Bonbon. But, did you mean that even if she's our dog, we could still lose out?"

While they spoke, Akara combed his hair and made sure his collar was not rumpled. "You better watch the road," he said, taking the iPad. "Hi," he said, "I'm working the case with Dr. Richards. My name's Akara."

Dee Dee was impressed. "Well, Akara, the dog's chip was removed. Somebody took a scissors and just cut the chip out of that poor little thing's withers. You're not gonna have an easy time. A young chihuahua female? At an animal shelter's price? This won't be an adoption line you're in. It will be a line of owners."

"What's the difference?" Akara asked.

"If it were an adoption line the dog would have to be spayed. But an owner with a breeder's license gets the dog intact. She's got a bad leg, but that won't interfere with her breeding potential. You ought to go check her out at the animal shelter."

"Can you give me that address, Dee Dee?"

"What do they call you for short, Akara? A.K.?"

"Sometimes they just say, 'Kalash.'" Akara and Dee Dee giggled and then she gave him the address of the animal shelter in Hagerstown.

"Thank you, Dee Dee, and please, thank Vivian again for us. You two have been wonderful."

"Let me know how you make out," she said just before she disconnected the call. "Let me give you my private cell number."

Akara recorded the number. "I'll certainly keep you in the loop."

"I guess the first thing for us to do is to be certain that she's Bonbon," Carla said. "And then I guess we have to call Tom Alardi."

It was near closing time when they arrived at the shelter. Late-comers, looking for Christmas presents for their children, had crowded into the registration office of the shelter. A harried security guard was trying in vain to keep them in line in the order in which they had arrived. The clerks announced defiantly that at 5 p.m. the shelter would close.

They were entitled to spend Christmas Eve with their families, too. But nothing seemed to help. Akara took Carla by the arm. "There's got to be a back door. Let's go out and find it. At least we know the guard's out front."

They left the office to go outside and walk to the rear. A quonset hut building behind the office seemed to be the logical place to find the caged animals. Carla and Akara entered an "employees only" door and walked through the aisles past the individual big dog pens and continued on to the stacks of cages for the small dogs. There, in the last cage, was Bonbon. The dog yipped and jumped at the gate trying to get out and Carla burst out crying and tried to open the cage.

"I wouldn't do that!" a guard cautioned. "You two got a ticket to be back here?"

"No," Carla said. "But this is our dog."

"Yours and a dozen other people's. When this dog is ready to be released on Wednesday you can present your case for ownership. Right now you can add your name and phone number to the list." He handed her a clipboard for #548 Female Chihuahua. Pure breed. 1 year. Carla wrote out her name and phone number with Akara's number as a secondary line.

"Who sent you here?" the guard asked.

Carla had already endured too many lies to be dishonest. "Mrs. Marquis," she answered.

"Dee Dee, the widow, or the old one, her mother-in-law?"

Akara turned and stared happily at him. "The young blonde one... Dee Dee... the widow."

"Good gal, that Delores. Tell her I said, 'Hello.'"

Beryl checked a few custom furnishing stores in Baltimore, asking who made their antique replicas. She got their names and addresses, but she had no time to run them down. Before noon she returned to the motel to tell George that she had to head back to Philadelphia. "I'm scheduled to wrap presents and to help prepare to serve dinner at the Hospice. Alicia Eckersley is waiting downtown for me to pick her up. We'll wrap them there and then deliver them to Camden. A bakery will roast the turkey but we've got to fix all the additional foods. Sorry, I must go." She paused in the doorway. "Are you going to be all right?"

George grunted. "It only hurts when I laugh. Say hello to the gang for me."

"Merry Christmas, Big Guy."

"Bah Humbug!"

Alicia Eckersley's personal charity was the *Christ the Savior Hospice.* She had gone over each patient's "most likely to be pleased by" Christmas gift list with the priest; but after discovering that most of the patients wanted new slippers and pajamas for Christmas, she ordered new slippers and pajamas for everyone and made Father Willem sit down again and create a new list. He was delighted to see Beryl come through the door with Sensei and Alicia Eckersley.

Sensei approached him stealthily. "Could I speak to you privately about a private matter?" Sensei asked. Willem practically leapt out of his seat. "Of course. Let's go back to my office... or if you'd like to step outside for greater privacy?"

Sensei led the priest outside. "I got two tickets to the Eagles-Giants game for next Sunday in New York. Wanna go? I drive up and back on the same day. Kickoff's at 1 p.m."

"What's that? The 30th?"

"Yep. It's not New Year's Eve."

"How late before we get back?"

"Seven or Eight. I'll pick you up at 9 a.m. I'm goin' nuts worrying about Sonya. I've got to keep occupied or I'll lose my sanity completely."

"Sonya? Listen, I've recently talked to a friend at Interpol who owes me a favor. Do you want me to send up a flare?"

"I've already tried them. They got nothing and I don't want to press. She works undercover so much that making inquiries may start people talking and jeopardize her position. Listen, it's Christmas Eve for God's sake. Why don't you take that collar off and we'll go shoot some pool and have a beer. The women are here. You're covered."

"I'd rather play shuffleboard. Two of the cleaning gal's boyfriends hang out at the pool hall. I'll go tell Mrs. Eckersley that you're quite upset and I need to counsel you. Beryl will know about Sonya. She'll fill her in."

While Carla celebrated Christmas Eve with George in a Baltimore motel, Akara Chatree was in Hagerstown, helping Dee Dee Marquis decorate a Christmas tree that she hadn't thought she would bother with this year. She had been a widow only ten months, she explained. "Motorcycle accident. No children. Everyone tries to fix me up, but I don't feel like being fixed up."

"If it ain't broke," said Akara, finding the opportunity he had been looking for, handed her a jewelry box he just happened to pick up as a token of his "firm's" gratitude, "don't fix it." The box contained a gold choker that Akara enjoyed fastening at her neck.

He was still hanging tinsel when Tom Alardi called to tell him that there would be a meeting of the law enforcement principals at the animal shelter in Hagerstown on Wednesday morning, 9 a.m. sharp. "Are you going to be around Hagerstown Wednesday?"

Akara turned to Dee Dee. "Am I going to be in Hagerstown Wednesday morning?"

"I thought we could visit some of my old friends tomorrow... you know... holiday cheer and all that. I've made fruit-cakes that I'd like to deliver. So, sure, if you want to be."

Akara did not drink alcohol but he found himself getting high on Dee Dee's fruitcakes which were loaded with rum. He remembered the paramilitary friends of the lovely Dee Dee. "That might be interesting," he said. Feeling more amorous than brave, he affirmed it. "Yes, I'd like that."

Tom Alardi came from his office to the motel. As he parked he noticed two familiar drug-scene thugs emerge from the office and head down the walkway towards Akara and George's rooms. On a hunch, he went into the office and showed the clerk his identification. "Who were those two guys who just left here?" he asked.

The clerk did not know who they were. "They wanted to know George Wagner's room number. I told them it was 16 - which is the room he and his associate took and he's officially supposed to be in. He's actually in Room 18, the room a fellow named Akara Chatree is registered in."

Alardi thanked her and hurried down to room 18. The two men had managed to get inside room 16. "I'm calling 911," he whispered to George. "Two thugs are inside the room Beryl and Akara are using. Maybe the two guys are the ones who zapped Ms. Pemberton. They ain't there to wish you Merry Christmas."

Tom also called ADA David Riordan who was happy to get away from his in-laws and came immediately. The police had the two men cornered in room 16.

Riordan took charge. They had broken into the room and that, alone, was enough of a crime to hold them. He read them their rights as the police took them away.

"Now," Tom Alardi counseled Carla, "It's great that you found Bonbon. But we've got a long way to go. They'll ask you to prove you owned the dog by telling them where you bought it. What can you say? When they find out it belongs to Roland, they'll contact him and you will have done nothing to advance your case. Hagerstown is in Washington County. I've already set up a meeting at 9 a.m. on Wednesday morning. Dave Riordan and an ADA from Washington County will be present for an ownership demonstration... one that will at least convince Riordan that his information from Roland is bogus. We must insist and prove that the dog was a gift. Maybe we can get the charges dismissed before they're even filed." He sighed. "What else have you been doing?"

"Akara gave me pictures of old vans and I picked out the one I thought it was. He cross-referenced the van owners with the custom furniture makers and we checked out three of them. We've got three more to go."

"He cross-referenced them? I don't even want to know; but now that I do, I cannot countenance the invasion of county records - if that's what's involved. Carla, you just stay at the motel and enjoy your holiday while taking care of Wagner. Akara is in good hands in Hagerstown. He'll be meeting us at the animal shelter on Wednesday morning. Well, a Merry Christmas to you both. I've got a family to get home to."

TUESDAY, DECEMBER 25, 2012

Tom Alardi could not resist calling Akara in Hagerstown. "I wanted to wish you Merry Christmas and give you some news."

Akara rolled over. "Same to you. What's up?" he asked.

"Plenty. I got a friend of mine to give me a few dozen new non-compete contracts and in preparation for our Christmas Party, I rolled them up and tied a red ribbon around them and gave them to every human being who works in my office. I had Christmas bonuses in envelopes in my desk. I waited to see who'd sign and who'd balk at signing.

"Gus Mellon, as expected, balked. He gave me a bullshit line about there being no necessity since he was thinking about retiring anyway. Guardino signed immediately. I assigned him Gus's corner office and gave him a big bonus, too, that I told him to keep quiet about. He was pleasantly surprised. I was grateful.

"Then my three other associates came into my office and signed, so did their secretaries. Gus's secretary and a couple of para-legals wouldn't sign so I gave them good severance packages and let them go. I feel like a new man. I want to hire you. You can name your price. I need somebody here who understands this computer stuff. George is right. It's a new age we're into."

"Thanks for the offer, but I've taken up the cloth, so to speak. I have a congregation of Zen Buddhists I serve up in Philadelphia."

"What about one of the guys in your hacking club?"

"I'll ask and if anyone's interested I'll have him or her call you."

Because Sensei had to work so hard and therefore had no time to think, Christmas Dinner at the hospice was pleasant for him. Beryl was exhausted. They cooked the entire morning and set the long dining room tables, decorating them festively. At noon, Sensei went to get the turkey from the bakery, and then he and Beryl began to wheel patient after patient into the dining room, or carry trays to the rooms of those who could not leave their beds and often stay long enough to feed each patient who needed help. A line of homeless people had spontaneously formed outside, and they fed them, too. They were assisted by volunteers, but it was still a long process. The dinner was not concluded until 4 p.m.

As they headed home, Sensei said, "I'm really glad I went and did something nice for somebody else. There was about ten minutes there... during the afternoon I think it was... that I didn't actually think about Sonya."

"I was all set to roast a small turkey yesterday and serve it cold with cranberry sauce on sourdough bread today for Jack. It's still in my freezer. When George and Akara get back, I'll defrost it. We can have a belated Christmas meal together."

At Tarleton House, the Smiths and the Haffners exchanged identical presents: Lilyanne and the baby with her mother and father in a filigree sterling silver frame; and an old family photograph of Eric, his deceased sister, and the Haffners taken in 1991 also set in a filigree sterling silver frame.

When the baby was down for his afternoon nap, Lilyanne stared at him. "In the next few months I'm going to make important decisions. I wonder what they'll be." The question was a serious inquiry.

In the Baltimore motel, George was relieved to feel only extreme tightness in his leg. Only when he stood on it did he feel pain. He would hobble into the bathroom and then hobble back, more hopping than hobbling, to his bed. Carla brought movies that she thought would be of interest to him. *Fight Club, U.S. Marshal,* and *Gladiator.*

WEDNESDAY, DECEMBER 26, 2012

Promptly at 9 a.m. Tom Alardi and Carla, followed by a member of the Philippine consul's staff, arrived at Hagerstown's Animal Shelter to be met by Dee Dee Marquis and Akara. Dave Riordan and an ADA from Washington County had not yet arrived. Tom Alardi explained, "The Philippine consul's staff member is going to videotape the demonstration. Incidentally, the pre-trial conference has been indefinitely postponed."

As the consular attaché pulled into the parking lot, he called to the small group, "Are we early?"

Akara looked inside the office which was empty of everyone except a few clerks. "No. Everybody else is late," Akara answered, and the attaché laughed.

Riordan arrived and he and Tom Alardi talked privately. Riordan's assistant, camera in hand, joined them and quipped, "Hey, Tom. Was Tiffany invited to the feast?"

"Naturally," Alardi said, smiling at the assistant, "Tiffany is my biggest fan."

"Jesus," Riordan whispered to Tom, "Now it's spread to my office. What the hell is going on?"

"I've been cleaning house, Dave. I'm starting the New Year right. What was that old War slogan, 'Loose lips sink ships.'"

"You've got a lot of work to do," Riordan said.

Dave Riordan recognized Ruth Meyers, the Washington County ADA, who had just pulled into the parking lot. Dave waved to her as he stood in the shelter's doorway. "We can get the show on the road now," he announced.

Inside the office, Ruth Meyers presented her credentials and took charge of the proceeding. "I'd like to set this up properly. You're holding a lame chihuahua in the back. I want everybody out here to be spread-out and silent. I mean... no movement, no noise. Just stand there like statues." She looked at Carla. "You go to the far end of the room," she instructed. "When everyone's in place and the photographers–" she gestured at Akara and Dee Dee; the consul's staff member; and at Riordan's assistant - "are ready, we can ask one of the clerks to bring the dog in and set her down in the doorway. That's all."

As the two photographers got into place, Alardi whispered to Riordan, "If that dog runs to Carla Richards, you've got a liar on your hands and maybe we won't have to go through the red tape of getting an old lady to make a statement in Pennsylvania. And you ought to look into the Melbourne's kid. That's your dog snatcher."

The clerk brought Bonbon to the doorway. Except for shivering, the little dog stood motionless in the doorway, sniffing the air. Then she turned and ran so quickly to Carla that she jumped from the floor up onto Carla's abdomen and Carla had to catch her to keep her from falling. The dog began to lick Carla's face and neck as she squeaked pitifully and wagged her tail. "Bonbon!" Carla cried. "Bonbon!"

The dog continued to scratch at Carla as if she were trying to dig a hole in her neck. She whimpered and squealed in a frenetic greeting. Carla could not put her down. The dog was not controllable.

"I'm convinced," Ruth Meyers said. "What is wrong with the dog? Why is she bandaged?"

"Somebody cut the chip out of her and the wound got infected," the clerk explained.

"And her leg?" Meyers asked.

"Congenital," the clerk answered.

"I want you to advise anyone who claims ownership of this dog of the penalty for perjury. They will have to sign a document saying that this is their dog and they'll have to prove where they purchased the dog. Tell them about the criminal charges and the fine that will be levied if they lie on that affidavit. Ok, Dr. Richards, the dog is yours... unless there is a serious counter-claim filed... and then that will have to be adjudicated. You understand."

"Yes," Carla said, "but I have no way to keep her permanently and I'd really like to honor the ladies who work at the hospital here - the one for children with bone problems. A child with a leg problem will fall in love with Bonbon and heal much faster. So what I'd like to do is take Bonbon to the hospital and integrate her into the environment gradually... every day for a week or so. Would that be all right?"

Riordan, Alardi, and Meyers looked at each other approvingly. The right decision had been made. Riordan said, "If that's ok with the folks here, I see no reason why you can't bring the dog up here every day. But the case is still open!"

The hospital was called and a nurse's aid came to the shelter to get the dog that was then being chipped in the hospital's name. "Would you mind calling her Bonbon? Her owners, Winifred and Daphne Buehler, would like that. She was their 'delicious little pup.'"

"Bonbon it is. You can introduce her to the children," the office manager said.

As they left the shelter, Riordan reminded Alardi that more serious charges were still being considered against Carla. "A lot of property disappeared after she began to visit the Buehler household. Important property. The dog's preference for her does not absolve her of larceny or, for that matter, homicide."

Riordan and his assistant returned to Baltimore and Ruth Meyers went to her office.

Tom Alardi followed Akara who, with Dee Dee, followed the nurse's aid, Carla, and Bonbon to the hospital.

In the hospital lobby, Alardi conferred with his other client, Akara Chatree. "Dinner was great yesterday. Gus cancelled. I'm feeling really good about my office staff. Finally. And I owe it all to you. Thanks. Tell Carla she's paid in full. I'm giving 10Gs to Wagner.... Pain and suffering for that dog bite. I'm also picking up his motel and medical tabs."

Akara took Dee Dee out to brunch. She was due to go on duty at the hospital but she used her liberal break-time to tell Akara about the many differences between an Uzi and an AK-47. Akara said he was fascinated.

Another chihuahua was playing with the children. Bonbon was so happy that she played with the dog and her new "owner" - a boy who had just lost his leg to bone cancer. After an hour of play, it was time to take Bonbon back to the motel. She was still not as strong as she should be.

They returned to the motel bringing "forbidden" meatball sandwiches to George.

The shelter had given Carla food for Bonbon, but she preferred to eat one of George's meatballs. "I have a way with the ladies," he said. "Riesling, my dear?"

With an expressed hope that Easter would be celebrated in Vienna, Erica and Hans bid farewell to Cecelia and Everett.

"It is odd," Cecelia said returning to the house after waving goodbye, "that I do not feel exhausted or particularly happy to see our guests leave. She wasn't a bad sort and we knew a surprising number of people in common... some I had quite forgotten about. She's an excellent gossip. I received more than I gave."

Lilyanne had also waved goodbye to them on the portico. As the car passed beyond Tarleton's gates, she re-entered the house and asked herself why George had not called.

THURSDAY, DECEMBER 27, 2012

The problem could be simply stated: George and Akara each had a vehicle and they each should have returned to Philadelphia. George, however, could not drive his pickup truck for another week, and since Akara was in no hurry to leave Baltimore or Hagerstown, they decided to spend New Year's in Maryland. There was still an investigation to conduct.

Carla had correctly supposed that the maid would not be at the Melbourne's house, but she did not know if Barry, who was on a school break, would be home. No yellow Mustang was parked outside. "Now," Carla explained to Akara on their cellphones, "the alarm control box is inside the formal vestibule. Since they prefer to keep the door between the house and the garage locked, it's necessary to park and then to walk around to the front door. It's slightly inconvenient but," she laughed sardonically, "they say, 'Considering the potential for thievery in the area, taking a few extra steps to enter the home is well worth the effort.'

"As a matter of routine, the maid unlocks the front door and then punches the code into the keypad, disarming the system which uses a telephone line to communicate with the security headquarters. There's an option to rearm the system but the maid doesn't use it because she goes in and out of the house, emptying trash, and so on. She cleans until noon at which time she codes herself out and drives away."

Akara in his Corvette and Carla in George's pickup truck slowly cruised past the Melbourne's residence, circled the block, and then stopped in front of the house. Akara parked the Corvette and set his iPad on he dashboard, focussed on the front of the house. His hacker friend verified that he could see a clear picture of the house and said he'd keep Akara informed if anyone showed up. Carla parked the pickup behind him.

Akara told his friend, "We're ready to enter." Asked to wait for a minute, he said to Carla, "Maybe we'll get lucky today. All my research and I never considered animal programs for hospital kids. What is this world coming to when a gun-toting Mama from a paramilitary group can outthink a 16 server cluster? Do you know how many thousands of dollars worth of equipment I've got stored in my room in the Temple? And Sensei just walks away from the place, leaving it open. 'People want to pray and meditate,' he says. I've often gone out to find him gone and the place open."

"Well, if it's ever stolen, you know who you can replace it with."

"Sure! Her husband taught her how to shoot. Her friends all rave about what a great shot she is. She can also shoot a bow and arrow. She's won trophies. I'll have to start picking my teeth with a stiletto... and get a pit bull for a lap dog. I'm beginning to doubt George's assurance that we've entered a new age of technology. I'm getting a strange feeling that some Robinhood is gonna lead us into sails, snares, arrows, samurai knives and Colt Peacemakers. And I don't even know how to tie simple knots."

His friend got back on the line. The alarm service was shut off.

As they approached the front door, Akara said, "See if they still keep a key in the fake rock. I hate picking locks!"

Carla picked up the phony rock and twisted it open. A new and probably unused key was nestled in its foam rubber bed. She handed it to Akara who unlocked the door and ushered her into the house. No lights shone from the control panel. The system was dead.

They headed immediately for the basement. The door to the basement was locked and Akara got his first chance to display the lock picking skills George had taught him.

Once they were safely in the basement, Akara decided that the logical place to look for paid invoices for custom furniture would be, in Roland's system, "Miscellaneous Expenditures." It was not.

Carla found the recipients' names of flowers that had been sent by the aunts to funeral parlors and hospitals. She recorded them in a paper tablet. Akara asked, "What would Roland be likely to call the custom made furniture?"

"I would think he'd pay cash and burn the paper evidence."

"You are no help."

"Get his bank statements and find withdrawals for September and October. Or see if he ever recorded anything about a Windsor chair... or got a formal appraisal or something. He could have forged provenance papers and advertised it for sale."

"Let's look for an insurance policy on anything in storage."

Roland Melbourne was determined to have a long talk with his son. Barrington clearly had lied to him again. The boy was supposed to deliver the "non-papered" dog to a sleazy breeder and pick up a cash payment of $500. Roland, specifically, did not want to be associated in any way with the dog. The breeder would be able to neutralize the owner's chip. But Barry had returned without the dog or the money. The pup had escaped, he whined, when he had stopped to let it urinate by the side of the road. His tale was so convincing that Roland and Sybil actually tried to comfort the boy.

But that morning, the vet who had originally cared for Bonbon had heard the story about the lame chihuahua that had had its microchip scissored out of its withers. He related the details of the "law enforcement" test at the Hagerstown Animal Shelter. "What is going on?" the vet asked. Roland replied that he did not know but said he'd sure as hell find out.

But Barry had known that the dog was worth much more than $500 and that his father was paying for anonymity. Barry therefore took a sharp cuticle scissors and performed the surgery himself. He intended to sell the dog for $1000 to a breeder and then, when that plan didn't work out, he'd sell it at a discount to a friend whose chihuahua female had died giving birth to a litter that another dog had nursed. The papers were still good for the dead dog and Bonbon would have a new name.

When he arrived at his friend's house, he tried to wrap a blanket around the dog and the wiry little dog jumped out of his arms and ran away into a neighbor's wooded back yard.

He tried and failed to find the dog; and then he returned home, appearing to be so distressed by Bonbon's disappearance, that Roland and Sybil believed him.

And now Roland knew that his son had lied yet again.

When the 'sleazy' breeder called wondering when the dog would be delivered, Roland said, "The deal is off, I'm afraid. My son had an unfortunate accident while he was delivering the dog to you. Please accept my apologies."

And now, several weeks later, everyone seemed to know about the test in the animal shelter, a test, the Vet had told him, that had been officially filmed in the presence of several members of the district attorney's office. Roland, not welcoming law enforcement into his business in any capacity, called his son in the boy's Hagerstown apartment and said that he would meet him at home immediately and that he could expect changes... major changes... in his lifestyle.

Instead of finding Barry's yellow Mustang in front of the garage, Roland saw a bright red Corvette and a dark blue pickup truck at the curb in front of his house.

The Corvette obviously belonged to one of Barrington's many drug-dealing friends. What was going on that they needed a pickup truck? Was some of his own furniture being taken? He called Sybil and continued driving past the house.

"I'll be there in ten minutes," Sybil said. "What is he up to now?"

Roland related his conversation with the Vet and then waited at the side street turn-off that his wife would use. As soon as she saw his brown Toyota, she beeped her horn and slowly proceeded as Roland followed.

"What else can he be after?" Sybil whined to her husband on her cellphone. "He's already hocked my jewelry. I'm wearing the watch you got me for Christmas." She pulled up onto the driveway.

"It's all right, Syb. We'll get to the bottom of this right now!"

In the basement, Akara's friend notified him that two Toyotas had just pulled into the driveway.

Sybil reached the front door first. The door was ajar. "The system's been disarmed," she hissed at her husband. "Where's the Mustang? Did you see his car anywhere?"

"No. What the hell is he doing with a new Corvette?" Roland brushed past her and called, "Barrington! Barry!"

Sybil looked through the downstairs. The cellar door was shut but she did not notice that the locking pin had not been released. She pointed up. "Try the attic!" Both of them bounded up the staircase, calling their son and demanding to know what was going on. Roland scampered up the ladder and saw immediately that no one was in the attic.

Carla and Akara considered their escape. As soon as they heard Roland and Sybil rush upstairs, they waited a moment, and then, crossing quietly on the carpets, ran to the front door. As they exited the house, Carla carefully pulled the door shut behind her, and Akara instructed his friend, "Activate the alarm now!"

Sybil and Roland did not hear the front door open and shut; but as they rushed down into the living room, they saw that the basement door was open. "I'll check the basement," she shouted, running to the basement. She descended half way down the steps before she was able to see that no one was there. "They've gone!" she shouted at Roland. "They were here! They left file drawers open and papers out!"

Roland had rushed out the front door without punching in the code. Sybil followed. They both tried to run after the pickup truck to get its license number, but both vehicles had driven too far down the street, their license numbers no longer readable.

While they returned to the house, the activated alarm system was beeping a notice that the front door had been opened without the code having been punched into the control. A security company car arrived at their address. They were not known to the security officers and had to prove their identity. The home office revealed that they didn't have a history of false alarms and the guards, assured that the Melbournes had made a simple oversight, accepted their apology and left.

To Sybil and Roland it was obvious that only someone who knew the code could have entered and left the house without setting off the alarm. Carla and a new red Corvette did not go together. Barry and a new red Corvette did. And what did he need a pickup truck for?

"They didn't steal anything," Roland said quizzically. "What the hell could they have wanted to haul away?" He looked through some of the files that had been removed.

The awful truth occurred to Sybil. "Barry must have overheard us talking about the storage locker and where we kept the combination; and now he's got the combination to it! His Mexican connections could have figured out the *derecha - izquierda* "d" and "i" for right and left!"

"My God! They're heading for the storage locker!" Roland gasped. "Let's take my car," he called as they rushed from the house, this time remembering to punch in the security code.

Akara had seen the sequence of numbers written in pencil on the outside of a folder, but the numbers meant nothing to him.

Fearing that they might be followed by security personnel, Akara led Carla into a fast food entrance line. He had just paid for his food at the window when he saw Roland's car speeding past. He called Carla's cell. "Roland just passed here. I'll follow him and you follow me." He entered the highway and followed the Toyota.

Carla was nearly a block behind him as he was a block behind Roland. They came to the edge of Dalton Creek. A building that accommodated both a storage locker and a truck rental facility stood alone at the side of the highway. Roland exited, deliberately moving to the left side of the exit ramp so that he could cross over the highway. It was clear that this was where they were headed. Akara went into the right side of the exit ramp and turned off the highway, parking in a gas station. He put gas into the Corvette while he hoped and waited for Carla's pickup to follow him.

He had paid for the gas by the time she pulled into the station. "Follow me!" he called. "They must be at the storage locker over there."

They went across the overpass and parked their cars as inconspicuously as possible near the front of the office. The Toyota had already gone back into the alleyways of the rows of lockers. Akara saw an open locker and the brown car parked outside it. Using his iPhone he began to film the activity. He noted the locker number as Roland stood outside it, while Sybil drove the Toyota to the front parking lot. She sat in the car and made a series of phone calls. Then she walked to the alleyway, and Roland left to go to the truck rental section of the complex. The Toyota remained parked in front of the building. Akara and Carla watched as Roland entered the truck rental facility, and Sybil remained in front of the locker, talking on the phone.

Roland left the building carrying papers and climbed into a truck that was parked at the side of the front lot. As he pulled up to Sybil in the rented truck, she continued to speak to someone.

The truck backed-up to their locker. Carla peeked around a corner of the facility. "They're taking the antiques out of the locker and putting them in the truck! Shall we call the police?"

"And tell them what? That people who've rented a locker are moving its contents? You weren't formally charged. There's no crime on the books! Let's just video them."

Carla protested. "There was some kind of complaint or I wouldn't have just been put through hell!"

"They've got to be taking the furniture somewhere. We can follow and find out where."

"That's probably what Sybil was doing on the phone... lining up a place to put the stuff."

Akara had an idea. "I've got George's GPS software in my iPad. Get the transmitter out of the pickup, and make sure it's turned on. It doesn't have a magnet attached so you'll have to stick it under the seat of the Toyota!"

Carla ran to the pickup, got the GPS transmitter and casually walked up to the Toyota that was still parked in front of the office. She opened the passenger side door and carefully placed the device under the seat. She turned and looked at Akara who signaled with an upturned thumb that he was receiving the signal. She casually walked back to Akara. Together they waited to see what would happen next.

It required less than half an hour to load all eleven pieces onto the truck. Sybil had taken the drawers out of all the pieces to lighten them and Roland was easily able to use the dolly and the ramp to get the pieces onto the truck bed.

Sybil got into the Toyota and led the way for Roland to follow in the truck. When they had gone half a mile up Highway #140, Akara got into the pickup and with Carla driving they proceeded northwest on #140. Akara followed their changing coordinates on his iPad.

"Will they be going to another storage facility?" Carla asked.

"I doubt it. It's easy for law enforcement to get into a storage locker, but it's tough to invade someone's domicile. They'd need a warrant and some pretty strong probable cause."

"What made you so sure to put the transmitter inside the Toyota? How did you know they wouldn't have gone together in the truck?"

"She's not the type to conduct business in a truck. It wouldn't look legit if she met a real estate agent or an owner with a rented truck filled with antique furniture. They probably had to find an isolated place that was ready to let. They'd need to move into it immediately so that they could unload the stuff. He'll probably just keep driving past her while she talks to the owner or agent and then she'll call him when it's safe to come back."

"Makes sense."

As Sybil and Roland turned off the highway in Winchester, the pickup followed them. Finally the Toyota stopped outside an old farmhouse. Akara could see that the truck continued to drive past the car. Carla pulled off the road under a group of trees so that they could watch. Sybil got out of the car and was greeted by another woman dressed in a business suit.

A half hour later, the woman departed and Sybil returned to the outside of the Toyota and made a phone call. Immediately, the truck appeared, coming from the opposite direction.

Akara recorded the coordinates. "I'd love to drive by the place," Carla said, "but we just can't risk it. It's after 4 p.m. now. It took them half an hour to load the stuff into the truck. It'll take longer for them to put it into a house, assuming they don't just unload it in a garage, that is, if they have a garage."

"We'll wait an hour," Akara said. "That'll give them time to drive away without running into us."

Front steps and a porch made of bricks lent the house the illusion of structural integrity that it did not, in fact, possess. Sybil pulled up alongside the real estate agent's car and looked approvingly at the farmhouse. The two women shook hands and walked into the building as Roland drove past in the rented truck.

The farmhouse had once been the dwelling of the family who ran the farm, but they had prospered sufficiently to build a new house for themselves at the corner of the property that was nearest town. The farmhouse did meet the habitation standards for the temporary housing of farm laborers, but when the family invested in new farm machinery they only rarely needed to use it for laborers.

"We'd like to store some things in the house," Sybil told the real estate agent when she called her from the storage locker. "We have no intention of living in the building."

"Did you plan to store the things upstairs or in the basement?" the agent asked in a worried tone that she could not conceal.

"No, right on the ground floor. We have a proper residence. But my husband would like to keep a few cabinetry things there where he could come and work on them on weekends. He's one of those tinkerers. Why? What's wrong with the upstairs or the basement?"

"You never can tell what will happen in a rainstorm. I wouldn't want the roof to leak on something you valued and, by the same token, I wouldn't want a flood to damage anything you kept in the basement. We do get our share of hurricanes, you know." She quickly changed the subject. "The house is heated by an oil furnace and I'm afraid you can't hook up more than a 110 little air conditioner. But I don't see why you couldn't close off the living room and cool that room down if you wanted to work in it. You'll need butane for the stove if you want to cook. And I think I'm obliged to tell you that there's no insulation in the ceiling or walls. It's a very old house, as you can see. Built right after WWII. But the good thing is that it's never had an asbestos hazard."

She did not mention that the roof ventilator fan had fallen out permitting a large colony of bats to occupy the attic. No effort was ever made to discomfit the bats since they were such effective insect consumers. She also overlooked dozens of families of rats that gleaned the farmlands and lived in the cellar and a few families of opportunistic northern copperheads that shared the same space. "Did you plan to spend nights here?" the agent's conscience compelled her to ask.

"No," said Sybil, disdainfully.

Satisfied that her clients would not have to deal with any impediments to peaceful living, the agent assured Sybil Melbourne that she and her husband would love the privacy that the residence provided. She then extended a lease agreement which she and Sybil executed, and she accepted first and last month's rent and a security deposit that, under the circumstances, constituted chutzpah of the worst sort. She further agreed - and had it written into the lease - that she would have the electricity and water turned on the first thing the following morning if Sybil signed the application papers and provided a valid credit card number.

Sybil checked the windows and exterior doors. They were solid. The smell of the building, however, was oppressive. "What is that stench?" Sybil asked.

"The house may not be insulated," the agent said brightly, "but it locks up tight and I'm afraid that every smell that was ever here gets magnified in the stale air. If you leave the windows open you'll get a nice draft through. Here, I'll show you." With that she went to a front window, unlocked it and with little effort - since the old wood had shrunk - raised the bottom pane of the window. Then she went to the dining room and did the same. Immediately a cold blast of air came through the downstairs. "There," she said, "when your husband is ready to work, just have him open the windows for a few minutes."

Convinced that the house was secure, Sybil filled out the applications for the utilities, and provided her debit card which the agent ran through a machine that she happened to have with her. Sybil hurried the real estate agent through the process as quickly as possible. It was already late in the afternoon. It would take time to unload the truck and she and Roland could hardly work in the dark. The agent was happy to drive away from the place.

Ever mindful of the national importance of the furniture, Roland and Sybil brought the pieces into the living room, one by one. They worked quickly and were exhausted by the time the sun had dipped below the horizon.

It was twilight and with the front door open and dining room window open, the wind blew a clean cold through the house. Sybil collapsed on the bottom of the upstairs steps. Beside her on a pile of rags lay a 100 watt bulb screwed into a socket that was the terminal point of a long electric cord. She paid no attention to them. "Make sure the windows are shut and locked," she said to her husband.

Roland closed and locked the windows. "They're locked," he said. "How much protection the locks will give is another story. Shouldn't one of us remain with the stuff?"

"You can stay in this stench if you want to. I'm filthy and need a long hot bath. And you have to find out what Barry is up to. My God! When I think of all the promises he made after he stole the silver flatware and sold it for a pittance. What are we going to do about his lying! His stealing! He simply has no respect for anything. That boy is breaking my heart!"

"Now, dear," Roland said softly. "He's going through a rough patch. The best we can do is to keep him away from those thugs. They'll force him to give him these things if they find out where they are. So let's not lose our heads. They're probably at the locker now cursing us for having outsmarted them. We have to continue to stay ahead of them. Come on, let's go back. Remember... as soon as we get home, put that lease in a place he'll never find it. They were looking down in the basement, so be sure to put it someplace safe."

"Where?" she asked, as they closed and locked the front door.

Roland walked her to her car. "Not in the kitchen or a bedroom or my den. I'm thinking that if you got a black envelope and carefully taped it to the back of the TV they'd never lift the TV off the wall to look at it."

"Rolly," she hissed, "for God's sake! They'd steal the goddamned TV. It's plasma!"

"Oh, sorry. Well, there's a drawer in the coffee table. Tape it up onto the underside of the table so that even if they pull the drawer out and turn it over, they'll still never think of reaching in and feeling around."

"That's a good idea. I'll put it in a stiff piece of plastic and tape it good."

Satisfied that they had solved the problem of hiding and maintaining the secrecy of the hiding place, they drove to the truck rental place, returned the vehicle, and went home.

Night fell. Akara called George on Carla's phone. George demanded to know where they were. "I'm only calling," the young priest-detective said, "to see how you're feeling and to tell you that we found the antique furniture. Just go back to sleep. We'll be back tonight or tomorrow - as soon as we figure out what we're supposed to do." As George began to curse, Akara disconnected the call and called Tom Alardi. "Tom," he said softly, trying to conceal the triumph in his voice, "we've found the antiques."

"Where are they?"

"I'm not telling you anything on your phone. Remember? Leaks? Go out and find a pay phone and call me and I'll fill you in."

Alardi drove around for nearly half an hour before he found a pay phone. Akara and Carla had meanwhile checked into a Westminster motel and ordered a pizza and cokes for dinner.

Tom Alardi called. "What is going on?" As Tom heard the news, Akara was explaining all the laws he had broken to find the antiques.

"What the fuck do you mean? Your friends disabled the home alarm system of the Melbournes? You broke into their house? You rifled their files? You placed a GPS device registered to George Wagner *inside* their car? And this is good news? Where are you?"

"Carla and I are in Carroll County."

"Oh, Great. That's another goddamned jurisdiction. I'll have to call Dave Riordan immediately. Where specifically are you?"

"I don't know if I should tell you. You're scaring me. We found the antiques. Ain't that enough?"

"Where are you? Listen, Saint Akara or whatever your religious title is, you say they rented a truck. That truck has a GPS record which is back in the office of the place they rented the truck... which I'm guessing is next door to a storage locker company probably in Dalton Creek. How long to do you think it is going to take me to find out where the hell that truck stopped long enough to unload the furniture?"

"Oh. Ok. We're at the Economotor Lodge in Westminster. Room 27."

"I'll call Dave and get back to you. Now I have to find some fucking quarters." He slammed down the receiver.

Dave Riordan had just gone to bed. "I'm bushed," he said. "Too much company. The wife had an open house for her relatives. What's up?"

"Well, Dave. The furniture has been located... the original antique furniture. It's been moved into Carroll County."

"Well, Tom. What's the crime in that? Melbourne hasn't filed a phony insurance claim yet. There's been no complaint of theft formally filed. That was the motive for the homicide which we've just begun to investigate. What do you want me to do? Without a crime reported, I can't get a warrant. And how do we know what the stuff is? I'd have to see the furniture along with a credentialed antique appraiser to determine that these were the pieces that used to be in the Buehler house. Let me rephrase that. The DA from Carroll County has to make that determination. And if Carla Richards is charged with killing Winifred Buehler because she wanted to get her hands on the stuff, Roland will say that he intercepted her intentions to sell it by putting it there for safe keeping. Tom, ain't nothin' happening tonight. I'll make the calls in the morning when there's somebody there to answer the phone."

"I'll get the address from my client and call you first thing tomorrow." He got into his car and headed for Westminster.

Akara looked at Carla. "We really ought to get back George's GPS transmitter."

"Roland keeps his car locked."

"Even when it's inside the garage?"

"Probably not, when it's inside. On the driveway or street... definitely."

"Let's go." Akara called his friend, asking that he give him a five minute interlude of alarm-free time at the Melbourne residence. "I'll call you when I'm ready to make an entry."

It was close to midnight and the house was dark. "We have to enter through the front door so come along with me and get that key and I'll enter and go through the bolted door to the garage. I'll have to exit the same way and put the bolt back in position. It has to be fast."

Carla walked ahead of him to produce the hidden key which he took from her as he passed. He called his hacker's club friend. "I'm ready to enter." He gave the key to Carla who returned it to the fake stone.

Given the go-ahead, he entered the house. Carla moved in front of him, carrying a flashlight. She led him to the garage door and slowly drew the bolt back. Akara opened the door and the two of them entered the garage. The brown Toyota was unlocked. Carla opened the passenger's side door and reached under the seat to grab the transmitter and give it to Akara. She shut the car door as well as she could without slamming it and the two of them exited the garage as they had entered it. In five minutes they were on the sidewalk telling Akara's friend to reactivate the alarm system.

When they returned to the motel in Westminster, Tom Alardi was waiting for them. "I ought to run the two of you in. What the hell were you up to? I thank God that both of you are my clients."

"We heard how upset you were," Carla said, "so we figured it would be best if we retrieved George Wagner's GPS transmitter."

"Where was Roland's car?"

"In his garage."

"How the hell did you get into his garage?"

"Through the front door... same way we went before," she answered simply.

"Friends of mine shut of their security system," Akara said softly. "They've got an old, antiquated system."

"And how the hell did your friends shut it off?"

"Tom. It ain't hard to do. The bookkeeping system determines if your service gets turned on or off. It ain't rocket science."

"I don't want to know any more about it," he said. "This is the craziest thing I've ever heard of. Nothing... nothing in this universe is private anymore. We are a planet of spies. Mother Earth is in a cocoon of electronic signals and devices that are all transmitting shit about us." He kicked off his shoes and took off his outer clothes and hung them in the closet. "I ain't leavin' you two until somebody from the DA's office tells me we're not under arrest." With that he popped a pill, drank a glass of water and lay down on the room's other double bed.

George Wagner had had the same response to the news that "all was well and the furniture had been located" with the aid of his pickup truck. He called Beryl and insisted that she drive to Baltimore immediately if not sooner. She did and also arrived at his motel just before midnight. "We're in a holding pattern," George explained. "Make yourself comfortable."

FRIDAY, DECEMBER 28, 2012

It took awhile for three individuals sequentially to use the bathroom's many facilities. When everyone was finally dressed, Tom Alardi led the way to his Lexus and said, "We'll eat and then you can show me the place... and then I'll call Dave Riordan... maybe."

At 9 a.m. the real estate agent paid the fee at the electric company and had the service restored to the farmhouse. The light bulb at the end of the cord suddenly glowed with old 100 watt light. The morning was cold, but the rags that lay under the bulb immediately began to warm.

As Tom Alardi took the road that led to the farmhouse, they could see smoke in the distance. A fire truck clanged and blasted its warning horn behind them. Tom immediately pulled off the road to let it pass.

"Oh, Jesus," Akara said. "That's the farmhouse."

"We'll just stay back here. We are not firefighters. And we do not want to get involved. Tell me now. Did you have anything to do with the fire?"

"Absolutely not!" Carla exclaimed. "You are our alibi. We did not start any fire!"

"Oh," said Tom. "Good." He called Dave Riordan. "FYI," he said, "the missing furniture may have been somewhat damaged."

After he concluded his conversation with Riordan, he turned to the others. "Well, the fire company tells the utility companies to shut off the service. The owners or renters will be notified... assuming they're not inside the building." He found a "soothing" music station and said, "Now all we have to do is wait."

Beryl called Akara. "What is going on?"

"Can I tell Beryl?" Akara asked Alardi.

"Sure... why the hell not?"

Akara, pausing only to let George finish a series of cursing statements, proceeded to relate the activities of the past twenty-four hours. After saying, "We're on our way," George wanted to speak to Tom.

For that conversation, Alardi got out of the car. Fortunately, he was laughing and was in a surprisingly upbeat mood when he returned.

"What's so funny?" Akara asked.

"George reminded me of a Pennsylvania Dutch saying, 'We get too soon old and too late smart.'"

The fire department pumped a seemingly endless stream of water onto the burning building. It was a futile exercise. The wood was old and dry and riddled with worm and termite holes.

A real estate agent's car passed. The woman who drove it talked to the fireman in charge. Utility trucks came and went.

The building's windows had cracked open or had fallen out and huge flames protruded from the openings to lick the structure's exterior. Black smoke seemed to give birth to a hoard of bats that mysteriously flew out of it. Everyone stepped back to watch the tight formation of bats fly off like a streak of ink across the morning sky.

A loud creaking noise served notice that the roof was caving in. It fell, creating a firecracker display of sparks as the timbers struck the ground level. The fireman's hose directed its stream onto the pile of rubble and the clouds of smoke ceased to rise. Finally, men with pikes, picks and shovels moved through the ruins amid streams of water from the firemen's hose. And then the fire truck packed up and left.

David Riordan in his car and Beryl and George in her car arrived and parked beside Alardi's Lexus. Alardi and Riordan both insisted that no one should approach the building until someone from Carroll County arrived. In another ten minutes, the official, an elderly, weather-beaten man, arrived and assumed command. "It never fails," he said. "People don't use their heads. The service is cut off and then when they try to see if they've got any gas or electricity and turn the switch or the valve and nothing happens, they don't turn the switches back to an off position. Then when the service is restored, Boom!" He scratched his head and guessed the distance. "It's less than a furlong to the house," he said. "Let's walk."

"A furlong?" Akara whispered, confused by the measurement.

"One-eighth of a mile on a horse racing track," Alardi answered. "He's probably a ghost from *Havre de Grace*, an old and buried race track here in Maryland. Be careful. This old guy may break into a gallop."

George laughed. "I'll wait in the car. You guys can walk."

"Nonsense," Beryl said. "I've got heels on. I'll drive."

As she got back into the driver's seat, a brown Toyota followed by a silver one sped by them from behind. Everyone returned to Beryl's Explorer to watch and see what would happen when the Melbournes saw the farmhouse.

"I guess that as renters of the place, they were notified," Carla said. "They're the leaseholders."

"I smell law suit!" Akara said.

Tom laughed. "Whose? I can think of half a dozen plaintiffs."

From a distance they could see Sybil do an agony-dance on the road in front of the farmhouse. She raised her arms and spun around and sank to her knees. Roland bent over her in the misery of their *pas de deux*.

There was no crime tape around the property. It was a not even a smoldering heap of rubble. Everything was black and charred. Here and there a piece of wood with bubbles of heavy varnish - the kind rarely used today - lay amid the sopping grit of charcoal. Most of the rubble was the remains of old structural timber, lead pipes, and asphalt roof tiles.

"Somebody ought to collect the hardware," George said.

"That *somebody* ain't goin' to be *anybody* from this group," Tom Alardi replied. "The matter is no longer in our hands. Let's all go home."

The county official said ominously, "The fire was reported twenty minutes after the electricity was turned on. Maybe a hot wire contacted something flammable. Yep. It never fails." He began to walk to his car.

"Speaking as a citizen," Beryl said sadly, "what has happened here is a terrible loss."

"If only we hadn't pressured them to move the furniture," Carla said.

"If only they hadn't put it in the storage locker in the first place," Tom added.

"If only the sisters had donated the things to the museums sooner," Akara noted.

"Jesus," George grunted. "*What is this? A trip back to the Uncaused Cause?* Is it so hard to imagine that two old maids got a thrill out of sitting at a desk Washington sat at? And caring for the desk as they'd care for a child? They loved that goddamned furniture. People can cherish old things... things that have a special significance. It's not fickle like human love. Only death ends it. The sisters died and the antiques died with them. It was a kind of *Liebestod.*"

Riordan looked at the tumultuous grave. "*Requiem en Pace.*"

Everyone said, "Amen."

-30-